THE KHAN'S TALISMAN

....& Other Stories of Adventure, Mystery and Humour

By

JP Kerawala

Illustrations

Sonal Goyal
Sumit Sakhuja

UNICORN BOOKS

'Guldasta' is an imprint of
UNICORN BOOKS Pvt. Ltd., New Delhi-110002
E-mail: unicornbooks@vsnl.com
Website: www.unicornbooks.in • www.kidscorner.in

Distributors
Pustak Mahal, **Delhi**
J-3/16, Daryaganj, New Delhi-110002
☎ 23276539, 23272783, 23272784 • *Fax:* 011-23260518
E-mail: info@pustakmahal.com • *Website:* www.pustakmahal.com

Sales Centres
10-B, Netaji Subhash Marg, Daryaganj, New Delhi-110002
☎ 23268292, 23268293, 23279900 • *Fax:* 011-23280567
E-mail: rapidexdelhi@indiatimes.com

Branch Offices
Bangalore: ☎ 22234025
E-mail: pmblr@sancharnet.in • pustak@sancharnet.in
Mumbai: ☎ 22010941
E-mail: rapidex@bom5.vsnl.net.in
Patna: ☎ 3094193 • *Telefax:* 0612-2302719
E-mail: rapidexptn@rediffmail.com
Hyderabad: *Telefax:* 040-24737290
E-mail: pustakmahalhyd@yahoo.co.in

ISBN 81-780-6104-X

Edition : 2006

Printed at : Param Offsetters, Okhla, New Delhi-110020

Contents

1

The Khan's Talisman

It was late March in Kolkata and the last few days had been very hot and humid. But on this day a severe Nor'wester threatened to tear the city apart. Nor'westers, are seasonal storms that are generally welcomed as they cool down the city after the oppressive summer heat of Gangetic Bengal.

"Whew! How dark it's become, and it's not yet 3 PM," observed Shiv's cousin, Vicky. He had come down for a weeklong visit from Lucknow, but in two days, Shiv had had enough of him. He dreaded the remaining days he would have to tolerate Vicky. Shiv found him boisterous, and a big bully. But being five years younger, a foot shorter and some twenty-five kilos lighter, there was little he could do but to endure it.

Just then there was a loud clap of thunder and everything broke loose. A furious wind blew in from the Northwest, pelting the city with lashing rains.

"That's it," said a relieved Shiv, "no more football this afternoon." He hated the rough tackles Vicky always employed, often injuring him.

"No problem. Let's play wrestling." Shiv groaned knowing he had just thrown himself from the frying pan into the fire.

In the next hour, Shiv learnt that there were twenty-four different ways of being thrown harshly onto the mat; that when caught by an arm in a vice-like grip round the neck there was little he could do and that the bones in his body were there just to experience pain in different degrees.

"Look!" He cried eagerly, pushing Vicky off his back for the umpteenth time. "It's stopped raining. We can go out now."

"Great! Let's play football."

"But the grounds will be too slushy."

"No problem. What do you say to rugby?"

Dear God, Shiv thought, if playing chess with this maniac had proved too rough, two minutes of rugby and he'd surely be decapitated.

"No, no, no…I have a better idea. Remember you wanted to buy something from New Market? Let's go there."

"Good idea. I wanted to buy a knuckle-duster and a …"

Knuckle-duster? For a fifteen year old kid? Shiv sighed remorsefully, praying he would not end up being its first target. To further divide Vicky's prospective victims, Shiv informed his mother that they would spend the night at his friend Bablu's place.

Vicky got his knuckle-duster, a brass one, and immediately he went back his old self...a bully. In the crowded New Market, he purposely banged into smaller boys and instantly whirled round for a fight. It was only the timely intervention of Shiv that three innocent boys escaped a bashing

Disgusted, Shiv moved away from his cousin and walked on ahead. Behind him the leering Vicky kept flexing his muscles, displaying his new 'toy' to one and all.

"This boy needs to be taught a lesson..." thought Shiv angrily. Just then they were walking past Nizam Restaurant, the place where Shiv, in his earlier adventures, had discovered a magic cabin. He had used it to travel in time and space and had some of the most exciting times of his life. "...and I am the one who will do the teaching," he said aloud with a wicked grin.

He invited a hungry Vicky to have some chicken ***kathi kababs*** (chicken rolls), settled him at a table and went straight to find the old man who was always there to guard the magic cabin...Cabin No. 8. The old man instantly recognized him and smiled, his eyes lighting up.

"Still hungry for a new adventure?" Asked the guard.

"Not me," said Shiv hurriedly, remembering the narrow escape he recently had from the Chinese regime of the 35th century. "It's for my cousin." He saw the old man raise his eyebrows, obviously not liking the idea of an unknown

member. "I'll keep the cabin and the system a secret from him, and...it's very important to me," pleaded Shiv.

The old man kept quiet.

"Er...what place and year is it right now?"

"Mongolia...1183," replied the old man gravely.

Wow! Just what Vicky needed...a place and time just right for his cousin!

"...And is there any way you can ensure that he will be at the right place for the return trip?" Nothing would have suited Shiv more than marooning Vicky in Mongolia, but as they claim, blood is thicker than water.

"It can be arranged." Clearly the old man did not look happy.

"And... er... how long before he can return?"

"Minimum six hours. Thereafter the 'connector' will remain open till he returns."

Before the old man could change his mind, Shiv hurried back to Vicky and sweet-talked him into being blindfolded. Soon Shiv guided a blindfolded Vicky towards the magic cabin.

"Where are you taking me? I don't like this game..."

"Believe me, you are going to love this," said Shiv, positioning Vicky at the entrance of the cabin, ready to push him through. He looked towards the old man for the signal and seeing a grave nod, he pushed Vicky. But at the same instant, Vicky blindly grabbed Shiv's hand and both of them plunged into the cabin.

WHAM!! A blinding light, a floating feeling and they crashed onto the floor.

"Why in God's name did you grab me?" Shiv was seething with anger at finding himself next to Vicky…in a felt tent. He stepped outside and saw they were in the middle of nowhere…and by that I mean absolutely nowhere. There were huge stretches of plains surrounding them, and not a human soul in sight.

Vicky stumbled out, wrenching away the blindfold. He looked around him disbelievingly, blinked his eyes several times and slapped himself, looking blankly towards Shiv.

"Wha…Whe…How?" His eyes were bulging out of their sockets and his wide-open mouth had dropped to a level lower than a politician's morals.

"Nothing to worry about," Shiv reassured him quickly. "We've just travelled through time…and gone places. We're in Mongolia in 1183."

"Oh." Either it sounded absolutely logical to Vicky, or its meaning was totally lost within the maze of cells and tissues he dared to call 'his brain'.

Shiv cursed his luck at being thrown into another adventure; one he was not happy going through so soon after the last one. He looked about him as Vicky continued his display of a mortified boy. The 'connector' to this part of the world was obviously the rugged tent. But where was its keeper?

Shiv found him asleep on the other side of the tent. He was a very old man, bald with a long, drooping moustache adorning his face. He wore a coarse robe and a battered sword lay next to him. When Shiv woke him, he showed no interest. He mumbled something in a strange language, turned his back and promptly went off to sleep again.

Shiv turned back to Vicky who now sported one of the silliest grins he had seen. He was still circling round and round the tent, disbelievingly. "Wha… wher… how..."

"Its okay, you will get over it. Ah look, smoke! It's far away, but at least we will be amongst some civilization."

They walked for an hour across the wide plains towards the smoke.

"These must be the Steppes of Mongolia that we learnt about in our geography books," observed Shiv, gazing at the barren plains stretching endlessly in front of them.

"Uh, huh." It seemed that a cut-out of an open-mouthed grin was pasted over Vicky's face. For an hour, he had not spoken with the exception of some unintelligible grunts and exclamations, and was happy to follow Shiv wherever he went.

Suddenly, they heard the thunder of hooves, and an instant later saw four horsemen charging towards them. The horsemen, who seemed to have come out of nowhere, pulled up in front of them amidst a spray of sand and pebbles and hoarse cries of aggression. A spear came hurtling through the clear and crisp air and landed two inches away from Vicky's legs. The four men were extremely rugged-looking with slanted eyes and deeply tanned skin and were clothed in robes of fur. They rode the horses without any saddle or bridle.

The horsemen saw no retaliation from the boys who stood rooted to the ground unmoving, as though a game of 'I spy' was on. One of the men, the wildest looking one, jumped off his horse, swished out his long-bladed sword and ran towards the boys. He raised the sword with both hands and was about to bring it down on Vicky's head when Shiv finally found his voice.

"WAIT!!" He shouted. He raised his hands in a gesture of surrender, and signaled that they were unarmed. "We ... we... are...fr...friends," he stammered, frightened out of his wits. The wild man seemed to have leapt straight out of the pages of a book on barbarians.

The man halted in his attack, midair, and hesitatingly looked towards his mates for advice. There was some discussion and apparently it was decided that the boys should be taken prisoners. They searched them for hidden weapons, tied their hands behind their back and escorted them towards the direction of the smoke.

As they were marched off Shiv noticed a wet patch where Vicky had stood and hoped it was not what he thought it could be. Of course, by now Vicky's face had changed from the perpetual expression it earlier sported. Gone was the silly grin, gone was the blank look! Reigning supreme now, was the total expression of naked fear.

Soon they came upon the source of the smoke. It was a native settlement. There were about twenty tents made of either canvas, felt or fur. Horses were tethered at various posts. The tribe of natives looked dirty and rough. Strangely, most of them were outside their tents. They were all armed to the teeth, but somehow, instead of appearing threatening, they looked frightened. There were mild looks of inquisitiveness as the two boys were escorted in. But no one really bothered to make anything more out of it. Shiv was surprised at this luke-warm reception, as he was sure their different clothes and appearance would arouse much curiosity.

They were guided to a well-guarded tent and were pushed into it after their bonds were removed. A lone prisoner, a white man, already occupied the tent.

"Who are you?" The white man asked gently.

As Vicky was still speechless, Shiv replied, "We are from India. And you?"

"India? Never heard of it. Where is that?"

"Beyond the Indus river..." Suddenly Shiv remembered, "Our country is also called Hindustan."

"Ah, Hind!! I have heard of this great land, but it is the first time I've met someone from there. I am Father Joseph, a missionary from England." He got up and inspected them both. "But you are just boys. How did you travel so far?"

"Long story." Shiv worriedly turned his attention towards Vicky and tried forcing him to return to normalcy. "Don't worry Vicky, another few hours and we'll be out of here."

"I don't think so," intervened the Father. "I've tried to escape from here for the past two months, but these guards are very alert...and very cruel." He bared his back and showed dozens of slashes crisscrossing each other. "Ten lashes of the whip for each attempt at escape. And I've tried many times," he added with a sad smile.

Seeing the numerous scars, some fresh, dripping with blood made Vicky sit down on the ground, pale with nausea and eyes out of focus again.

"Why are these Mongols so heavily armed?" Asked Shiv.

"They are not Mongols", explained Father Joseph, painfully leaning back on the central post of the tent, "They are Tartars and they control the eastern parts of Mongolia. They are well armed as they are expecting trouble from the Mongols."

"War?"

"Yes, the Mongols are at war with the Tartars. These settlements will simply be demolished in minutes by the Mongol army lead by their great warrior…Temujin. The Tartars poisoned his father and he has sworn revenge. Rumour has it he has already plundered half of the Tartar's territory and is now heading this way. They say he is the greatest Mongol leader ever, and he is only twenty one."

Temujin? Shiv failed to recall the name from his history books.

"They now call him," continued Father Joseph, "Genghis Khan!"

The sky, like a chameleon, was changing its colour as dusk ushered itself in. Without the warmth of the sun it started getting cold. Along with the dark and gloomy atmosphere, the mood of the tribe changed too as everyone huddled together, fearfully gazing far out into the darkness, almost as though waiting for the inevitable.

"It's very cold." Finally Vicky found his voice. "And I am hungry too. Shiv, why did you bring me to this place? Where is the restaurant and where are my chicken rolls? I feel like giving you a wallop right now."

The harsh hours till now seemed to have been overcome by Vicky, thought Shiv, as he noticed his cousin return to his normal self. A hard nut like him probably needed a much tougher lesson to reform and learn compassion.

"There are some furs in that corner," pointed Father Joseph. "Help yourself to them before you freeze. It gets much colder as the night progresses."

Soon it was totally dark, yet the lanterns were not lit. In wide-open areas like these steppes, a spark could be spotted a mile away. Even the fires were extinguished as it was better to be cold, than dead.

"Y...yo...you know, he is right," stammered Vicky, now looking bulky with three huge furs over him, "It is ge...ge...getting very co...cold here. Ca...can't we go home now?"

Shiv calculated that the minimum six hours they had to spend in this time zone were almost over by now. If they did manage to escape, they could return home to warmth and safety.

"We will have to wait for our chance."

An hour later, they heard the dull rhythmic sounds of hooves on hard ground. The sound was low, but ominous. It must have been some distance away, but the alarm had gone up. The whole camp was on its feet running blindly from one end to the other, looking for a way out, but banging into invisible walls. Running away from the camp would also mean sure death by starvation and cold as the steppes, like a dessert, is a never-ending stretch of land.

And then with a piercing scream, the marauding hoard of Mongols rode through the camp, their spears and arrows streaking through the dark night on their murderous paths, their swords and axes swishing angrily at anything that moved and their burning torches lighting every tent standing. The attack lasted just a few minutes and at the end of it an eerie silence reigned. Not a Tartar was left alive to tell the tale of the massacre. The three prisoners were now in the hands of the Mongols.

"*Bring them to me*!" A deep voice shouted in the dark. The three were once again bound and escorted out of the tent. Out in the open they expected fresh air with the cold weather, but it was the stench of death that hit their nose. It was so revolting it made them sick. They could see nothing save for the glare of burning tents.

"Ouch!" cried out Vicky as he stepped onto something round and toppled over. Though the guards shouted at him to get up he groped in the dark to feel the object he had stumbled upon. It was wet and sticky as he held it in his hands. A guard brought his torch closer and Vicky identified it.

"AAAAAHHHH!!" he screamed, again and again, finally dropping the object where he stood.

"What is it Vicky?" Shiv forced his way towards his cousin to calm him down.

"Its...its...a man's head!" Vicky answered and collapsed on the ground, oblivious to the world.

A few sharp slaps and Vicky was lifted off the ground by the two guards, and then half-carried and half-dragged to a circle of flames. Father Joseph and Shiv were already there.

Sitting in the center was the most striking man Shiv had ever seen, or even imagined. He stood barely 5'9" tall, which is taller than an average Mongol, and commanded immediate respect and fear. He looked very young and very agile. His black hair fell to his shoulders with the same defiance and royalty that his intense eyes displayed. His entire presence projected untamed arrogance and royalty.

Shiv's knees were knocking uncontrollably as he stood before this man, eyeing his unsheathed sword that was still dripping blood. The man studied them for a moment, and then abruptly walked up to Vicky. With a savage jerk, he pulled up Vicky's drooping head by his hair and shouted something. The sagging boy, his eyes almost bulging out of the sockets paralyzed by fear, wept in despair. In disgust the man pushed Vicky's head backwards, spat out a command, and strode away from them.

Even as the guards held them and started taking them away, Shiv saw a movement in the darkness. Somebody out of the glare of the flaming torches was crouching and creeping towards them. Shiv saw it was one of the Tartars taken for dead. He was walking in a staggering manner, and he held

something in his hands. It was an axe. Suddenly the man was running, his axe aimed straight for the man who had just walked away from them.

"LOOK OUT!!" Shiv screamed. Immediately a soldier pulled him down, pushing a spear at his throat. *"BEHIND YOU!!"* He warned again, pointing at the back of the leader. Without thinking the leader, who was still holding his dripping sword in hand, bent on one knee and swung it in a huge arch. It slashed through the stomach of the Tartar assailant, even as his own axe was poised to strike. The Tartar's guts and other organs gushed out and hung loosely outside his robe.

Vicky's lights promptly went off again.

There was a moment's silence after the unexpected attack. The leader looked at Shiv with a confused yet angry gaze. He once again gave a command to his men and walked on.

The guards released the three prisoners from their bonds and waited to escort them.

"Whew, that was close," said Father Joseph, helping Vicky revive and stand straight. "That was Genghis Khan!" He was looking over his shoulder where the leader had disappeared into the darkness.

"I'll take your word for it." Shiv too was holding Vicky up, who was trying to come to terms with what he had just witnessed. "But what did he order his men before the Tartar attacked?"

"To execute us! But you saved our lives. Now we are the guests of Genghis Khan,"

Sleep, naturally, was the last thing that would come to the three. They huddled round the fire with more fur around them as the Mongol soldiers went about their work of stripping the slain Tartars of all their possessions. Three guards still stood around them.

"How do you happen to be here?" Shiv asked Father Joseph.

"Not by choice, let me assure you." There was a twinkle in his eyes that promised a lot of humour and fun...though the craggy wrinkles around his eyes and the rest of his face told another story. "I was in North China for many years where I had set up a Missionary Outpost. Three months, ago a marauding army of Tartars invaded us and killed everyone. I was their only prisoner."

"How did you know of lands this far East? I thought in this age, Europeans were still unaware of Ind...er...Hind and China."

"What do you mean 'in this age'? You sound as though...anyway you forget Alexander the Great. He showed us the way. Today there are many missionaries in China, though not in Hind or even Mongolia."

"Another thing, I thought Genghis Khan would have a large army. Here I see there are just a few hundred warriors."

"They operate in groups. The rest of the army will surely be close by."

Soon the excitement of the day wore off and sleep stepped in...not a pleasant or peaceful sleep, but one filled with nightmares and the horror of human extremities. The penultimate thought in Shiv's mind was of his mother, and he was glad that she wouldn't be worried about his not returning home that night. How he was going to return even the next day, he had no idea. But his last thought was of a man whose ferocious eyes would tear the soul of a man apart, by just looking at him.

"Wake up, you lazy lout!" Vicky was up amazingly early. The trauma of the previous night had once again taken a back seat, as he was almost his normal self. "Whew, what a lot we're holed up with," he said gesturing towards the rough and dirty Mongols around them. "The sooner we are out of here, wherever that is, the happier I'll be."

Shiv shrugged off the heavy furs and looked around him. Gone were the dead bodies and other signs of the horrors of the previous night. "Look at the big fire," said Vicky brightly, "even the cold is gone."

"Don't go near that fire," warned Father Joseph. Shiv focused his eyes on the fire and understood why. They were burning the bodies of the slain Tartars. Around him the original camp had been demolished and the Mongol warriors were preparing to move on.

And then Shiv got the shock of his life. Spread out across the steppes, as far as the eye could see, was the actual army of Genghis Khan. There must have been tens of thousands of soldiers, and yet Shiv had not been aware of them till he saw them.

"They know of another Tartar camp, a real big one, a few miles eastward," informed Father Joseph. "I heard them talk last night. They want to exterminate that camp by nightfall, so they will ride out soon."

"Come on, come on," shouted Vicky playfully and jumped on a drowsy Shiv. He brought his arm around Shiv's neck and pinned him down. "Say 'uncle'," he demanded.

The next few moments Vicky was to remember till his last days.

Suddenly, two powerful hands caught Vicky by his collar and hoisted him high. A few loud shouts from them and Genghis Khan leapt out of a nearby tent, his deadly sword raised. Shiv wondered if he'd ever put it down. He charged straight at Vicky, ignoring the cries of plea from Shiv and Father Joseph. He was about to cut Vicky in two when he thought of another idea. He gave sharp orders and in next to no time two horses were placed, one on either side of Vicky. Ropes were flung out and one end of each rope was tied on a trembling Vicky's wrist, while the other onto the saddles of both the horse. Similarly his legs were tied, with the other end on each horse. Vicky was spread-eagled in mid-air and from his terrified looks it was obvious he had stopped thinking.

Next minute, the horses were geared up to charge in opposite directions. Vicky was about to be torn in two, by the most gruesome mode of death amongst the barbarians.

"***STOP!!***" screamed Shiv, running to his cousin and holding him up. "*PLEASE STOP THIS MADNESS!!*" he looked imploringly at Genghis Khan. "He is my cousin!"

Genghis Khan looked surprised not understanding what Shiv said. Father Joseph quickly translated, as all stood transfixed as though they were part of a photograph.

"But he tried to harm you. For that, he must die!" Genghis Khan said, and Father Joseph explained to Shiv in turn.

"No, he meant no harm. Please release him."

This must have been the first time anyone had had dared to oppose an order from Genghis Khan. Everyone stared in disbelief. Meanwhile, Vicky's arms and legs must have stretched by an inch at least as the horses stomped and snorted, struggling to break loose.

"Please Shiv, lets go back to that restaurant," whimpered Vicky. "I…I've had enough of this…and I promise I'll never lay a finger on you again."

Shiv was genuinely sorry for his cousin, so when Genghis Khan finally ordered Vicky to be released, Shiv simply hugged him out of pity. "Don't worry, we'll soon return home."

Vicky was shaking like a leaf in a storm as the ropes were removed and he touched ground once again.

Later, the three were escorted to Genghis Khan's tent. They all sat around the fire and Father Joseph became the medium for conversation.

"You saved my life last night," began Genghis Khan, "I am indebted to you. How can I repay you?"

"You already have," said Shiv, embarrassed at being the centre of attention, "by sparing our lives."

"Where do you come from?"

"From a land far away…Hind!"

"Ah yes, I've heard of it." Genghis Khan held a far away look as though picturing a vision. "I've heard it is a beautiful land and…very rich. After I complete the rout of the Tartars, I'll move south and capture China." He spoke matter-of-factly, as though in his mind he had no doubt about the authenticity of his statement. "Thereafter, I will cross the mighty mountains and sack Hind."

Shiv's blood turned cold as he heard the great general's plans. If he sacks India, that would change the entire history of his beloved country. It could become another lawless place where marauding tribes kill each other, and where peace and prosperity could never flourish. Not a place he would like to be born in.

"Please Khan Sir, don't invade Hind," said Shiv haltingly; worried he might displease the leader. "It's a peaceful country and the people are good."

When Father Joseph translated, the Khan looked hesitant, but only for a moment. "Is that what you want?" Asked Genghis Khan.

"Yes Sir."

"Then so be it. I shall not invade Hind."

"Thank you, Sir." Shiv was glad. History, as he knew, would not change. He felt that by nature this man seemed good. "Why do you wage war and bring misery to others?"

Genghis Khan thought for a moment and replied, "the greatest happiness is to vanquish your enemies, to chase them before you, to rob them of their wealth, to see those dear to them bathed in tears, and to clasp to your bosom their wives and daughters."

Shiv was shocked to hear this. With such ideology to live by, Shiv wondered if his earlier surmise of the man's nature was correct.

"But before we leave I must gift you something. Something that will remind you of me."

With that he unclasped an amulet from around his neck. "This is the talisman of my family. It is the tooth of a Siberian tiger, killed by my grand father. It has protected my family for generations. May it now protect you." said he placing the amulet around Shiv's neck. "And if anyone ever harms you," he said looking at Vicky meaningfully, "send this to me...and I'll come."

Vicky gulped hard and tried looking elsewhere.

Genghis Khan got up abruptly. "Enough of talk! Let's go and kill some more Tartars."

Within minutes, the entire camp was packed and mounted. Vicky and Shiv shared a horse, and were surprised when Genghis Khan ordered them to ride alongside him, right in the front.

"Not a good idea, I tell you, if a battle is on," observed Vicky, too scared to even glance towards Genghis Khan. Behind them, riding shoulder- to-shoulder and stretching for miles

on both sides, was the mighty army of Genghis Khan. It was the most awe inspiring sight Shiv had ever dared to dream of. There were more goose pimples on him than there were soldiers on horses.

A terrifying cry from the leader and they were on their way. Father Joseph was left alone, along with a month's provisions, to fend for himself on his way out of the steppes.

The horses moved at a light canter maintaining a close formation. As neither of the boys was used to riding, it was a very uncomfortable and rough ride. Particularly as in place of the saddle they were seated astride some thin rug. With each step the boys were jolted off the back of the horse by six inches, and then dropped back like a sack of potatoes, only to be instantly bounced up again. In two minutes, both were bruised black and blue.

"Ca...ca...can we...walk?" Vicky wanted to know.

"Ask...him." Shiv pointed towards Genghis khan.

Thereafter the ride proceeded in silence. They moved in the direction they had come from the previous evening and soon Shiv could see the 'connector' far in the distance. They passed a few miles away from it, but luckily no one's attention was drawn to it.

An hour later Vicky, who was sitting behind Shiv whispered in Shiv's ear, "I th...think...my ba...backside has fa...fallen off."

"And I th...think...I...I...will never see...anything st... standing str...straight again." The constant bouncing had definitely shaken every bone in their body. Shiv wondered if their bones would stay intact in their respective places, or would they clutter down in a pile at their feet, the minute they got off the horse.

"There they are!" someone shouted pointing towards the huge mound on their left. The mound was not high, but very wide…enough to hide a Tartar army of ten thousand men. Much, much larger than what Genghis Khan had expected. With surprise on their side, the Tartars attacked with the roar of a battle cry. As the Mongols shifted their horses to face the oncoming enemy they heard another blood curdling scream behind them. They turned round to see another ten thousand Tartars who had been hiding behind a larger mound, come tearing across the plains towards them. The Mongols were well and truly trapped.

"Pl…please, let's ge…get back to Ni…Ni…Nizams," implored Vicky softly.

"I think you are right. The connector is not too far, and we are mobile…actually, much more mobile than I'd like to be. But how do we get out of this trap?"

A loud command thundered from Genghis Khan and his army instantly split in two, one each to tackle the divided army of the enemy. As they charged in opposite directions, the spectacle was like Moses parting the sea. In the middle, like a lone sentry, stood the steed with the two boys on it.

"Now seems to be a good time to disappear," suggested Vicky gently guiding their horse to go the same way they had come from. Expecting to be spotted any minute and chased, the boys allowed the horse to move a little faster than a walk. There was no reaction from either of the warring party so they shifted gear to a gentle gallop. Soon they reached the outer limits of the two armies and again slowed down, still not knowing what to expect. Enemies had intercepted each other and a savage battle was on. Their last concern was of the boys escaping.

"Don't tell anyone," whispered Vicky still too nervous to breathe easily, "but I think we are in the clear."

A smart slap on the horse's rump and the charge was on. At full speed they galloped out of the war zone towards safety. After five minutes, Vicky dared to show his emotions. "YIPEE!! WE ARE FREE!" Neither of the boys complained of the foot-high bounce they were now subjected to.

It was easy to retrace their steps with the footmarks of a thousand horses to follow. Hope and joy returned to their hearts.

"Isn't he a beautiful beast," remarked Vicky, happily stroking the steed's muscular neck.

"I think we should spot the 'connector' within fifteen minutes," estimated Shiv, glancing all round him. But when he turned around to check behind them, his heart froze to ice.

"*There's someone chasing us!*" he shouted above the sound of the rushing wind.

"*WHAT?*" a white-faced Vicky threw a quick glance behind him and confirmed the news. Four riders were after them at a distance of about half a kilometre. But being master horsemen they were riding at the speed of the wind. It was obvious they would catch up soon. "Oh my God! We are done for."

"Who are they, Mongols or Tartars?"

"Must be Tartars, they are dressed differently. *"Come on you old horse, my grandmother can run faster on her crutches."*

Shiv was thinking fast. The connector this time was an open one, meaning there was no specific time when the channel between the two time zones would open, unlike his previous adventures. This time they will not be transported to the 21st century just entering the connector at the right time. That could only mean that the keeper of the connector at this end will have to do something to send them on their way.

"They've already reduced the distance by half." Came the latest report from Vicky. "Do something, Shiv, do something!"

"What? I cannot even…"

Suddenly an idea struck Vicky. "I know! Show them your tooth Shiv, show them your tooth!"

"…Okay…" Puzzled, Shiv leaned over on one side, turned towards the riders and grinned, stretching his mouth to show all his teeth.

"NOT THOSE, YOU IDIOT!! Show them the tooth Genghis Khan gave you. May be that'll scare them away."

"Oh." Shiv quickly removed the amulet and dangled it high above his head for a minute.

"Have they gone?" He asked hopefully.

"They've seen it...and...oh no, they're riding harder. They must want the talisman as a trophy. Quick hide it, or better still, throw it away."

But Shiv put it back around his neck. "Look! There's the tent. We'll make it for su..."

Just then their horse stumbled.

The boys were thrown off the horse, but even as they rolled both were up and running after the stricken beast. An arrow whisked past Vicky's ear and he started sprinting, as he never had. He overtook the horse, but kept running wildly. Shiv remounted the horse and went after his wayward cousin. Three more arrows zoomed past them as the horse found it difficult catching up with Vicky. Shiv made a quick mental note to encourage his cousin into entering athletic events when they returned home. They drew next to Vicky and in one smooth movement Vicky leapt up on to the horse, behind Shiv. An ace hurdler too, Shiv noted.

More arrows thudded close to them as the distance between them reduced further to just a hundred metres. Leading the pursuers was a huge Tartar astride a very large horse, and it was him that the boys were most frightened of. He looked powerful enough to tear a man to pieces with his bare hands.

"I think they want the damn Talisman," said Vicky, seeing the sudden ferocity in the eyes of their pursuers.

"Yeah, looks that way."

"So throw it to them. Maybe they'll forget about us," Vicky frantically yelled at his cousin.

"Never!"

As they neared the connector, Shiv desperately searched for the keeper…the very old man. He spotted him still asleep behind the tent. They needed his services desperately as without him they could not be transported back to the 21st century.

"*WAKE UP!! HELLO!! WAKE UP!!"* shouted puny Shiv, as loudly as he could. But they were still a hundred metres away and his voice barely woke the sleeping old man.

Vicky, always the one with clear and powerful lungs, took the cue and bellowed. ***"GET UP YOU OLD COOT!"***

The old man jumped up as though someone had shouted into his ears. "*Quick, get ready to send us home,"* Vicky shouted as an arrow brushed past his leg, ***"or I'll haunt you the rest of your life!!"***

They reached the opening of the tent at full gallop and jumped off amidst a spray of dust. The huge Tartar was barely twenty metres behind.

"Quick!" urged Shiv to the old man who was walking slowly towards the tent's end. "Get us out of here…*NOW!!"*

The boys plunged into the tent as the old man touched it, uttering something inaudible. They started swirling immediately, but before it could reach a crescendo a gigantic body jumped on them. Next instant they all crashed onto the floor, and into the cabin at Nizams.

When Shiv and Vicky returned to their senses, they felt a crushing weight on them. On opening their eyes, they saw the giant Tartar sprawled on top of them.

So terrified were they that not a sound came out of their mouths. They struggled and squirmed and set themselves free and leapt out of the cabin. Immediately behind them jumped out the enormous barbarian. The old cabin keeper stood there gaping at the sight, which did not meet with his approval.

There he stood, the giant, almost seven feet tall. His bare body showing rippling muscles, he looked around trying to gauge where he was and what had happened. A kind of skirt made of some dirty skin was the only clothing on his body, and hatred and anger the only expression on his face.

He suddenly bent down and snatched at the talisman on Shiv's neck. The thread broke as though it was not there. Grasping it in his hand, his eyes shone with victory.

"I told you to give it to them!!" Scolded Vicky. "We wouldn't have been in this trouble, if you had only listened to me. Now what are we going to do about him?"

Meanwhile, the crowded Nizam restaurant had stood up in unison, transfixed at the imposing sight of the barbarian in their midst. No one cried out and no one moved. A few crockery items did drop off lifeless hands and crashed to the floor at the sight of the amazing spectre. Yet no one dared take his eyes off him.

Suddenly the barbarian, who just couldn't fathom where he was and what he was supposed to do, removed his huge sword from its sheath, raised it above his head in one hand, with the talisman still clutched in his other hand, and gave a ear-splitting, terrifying war cry.

Next instant there was a stampede. Everyone made for the nearest exit and jumped out of it, be it the doorway or one of the nearest windows. The Bengali Babus, clutching their dhotis, the womenfolk with their hands on their frantically beating hearts and murmuring **'ooribaba'** under their breath, the restaurant staff and the management, all vanished out of sight in a split second.

Left in the restaurant were Shiv and Vicky, both now on the floor, the barbarian standing above them with his sword raised, and the old keeper of cabin no. 8.

"Pl…please do something," implored Shiv of the old man, "se…send him back…if you can."

The old man looked furiously at Shiv. "You don't deserve to be helped! Look at what you have done! Now the whole world will know of this cabin."

"I'll…handle that…somehow, but please send this…this brute back."

The old man gazed hard into the barbarian's eyes and instantly had him mesmerised. "In you go!" he commanded and the barbarian, his huge shoulders suddenly hunched and looking as harmless as a kitten, meekly walked into the cabin. Shiv saw his opportunity, ran and snatched back his talisman, jumping back in time.

There was a flash, a stifled cry…and the cabin was empty once again.

"Where did you send him?" asked Shiv getting up.

The old man checked his records and replied nonchalantly, "452 A.D., Italy. The year Attila the Hun raided it."

"Poor chap."

The customers who had fled were craning their necks to look inside the restaurant, found everything quiet and cautiously started coming in again. When most had returned and were insistently enquiring about the giant, Shiv stood up on a chair and gave a hearty laugh.

"Folks, sorry to have frightened you so much. My cousin here insisted he could mass hypnotise a group of people. So we had a bet, and he tried projecting an image of a giant barbarian in your minds. I must admit and accept that he has succeeded. Friends, what you saw was simply and act of illusion, so please just forget about it."

Vicky expecting a loud applause also stood up on a chair and bowed gallantly all around. First a curse was thrown at him, then some abuse and finally a barrage of parathas, raw eggs and other missiles were rained on him.

Later that day, a much changed and reformed Vicky played chess with Shiv.

After losing the fifth straight game and curbing innumerable urges and impulses to box his cousin's ears, he asked, "I still don't get it about our adventure. Did it all really happen or was that a part of the illusion too?"

"I'll suggest just think it never happened and forget about it."

"Oh yeah? Then what about the talisman Genghis Khan gave you?" Vicky asked fearfully. "Was that an illusion too?"

"What talisman?" Shiv had removed the amulet for a number of reasons and had placed it amongst his other 'trophies' from previous adventures. He didn't want to explain how he got it to his other friends and he didn't want to be kidded about it as it hung large and heavy on his little body. He also didn't want to risk losing it as it meant a lot to him.

Later he poured through his history books and finally found what he was looking for. In the middle of a chapter on Genghis Khan it was written, "And after conquering Mongolia he invaded China. When most of China was in his control everyone expected him to move further south, cross over the Himalayas and invade India (Hind, at that time). But inexplicably, to everyone's surprise, he turned his attention and army towards the west, and invaded Central Asia."

A smile played on Shiv's lips, as he knew he had played a part in saving his beautiful country's past, and in making history as we know of it today.

❑❑❑

2

The Power of a Prayer

When people pray, they do it with varying degrees of intensity. It could be with hands joined in prayer in front of a stone idol or a picture, but the mind busy with the days' happenings, and words chanted automatically and meaninglessly. Such prayers reach the ears of the idol, or picture, and fall down beside it, unfulfilled. Then there are prayers that are made with little show of devotion, but with such strength of faith and concentration that they penetrate the ears of the idol, or the photograph, and reach 'Him' directly. It is only such prayers that get fulfilled, and the people who pray with such intensity are few.

Children though, generally fall in this category. They have no doubts that their prayers will be answered. Their prayers are not about money or power, and are never filled with malice or ill feeling towards anybody.

One such child was nine-year-old Amol. He always prayed with his heart.

"Don't worry Father, everything will be fine now," He said, completing his prayers.

His father, Ram Gopal looked down at him and smiled sadly. He playfully tousled the little boy's hair, "I am sure it will son. I am sure it will."

But he knew his troubles were far from over. In fact, it might even get worse. He looked around the almost empty room that he and his family called 'home' and wept. He was a small farmer who had an average plot of land that he tilled all by himself.

Two years ago, he had taken a moderate loan from the local moneylender to get his daughter married. The interest the loan shark charged was so high, he could not keep up with the repayment of even the interest, let alone the original principal amount. Bhanu Singh, the moneylender, along with his tough goons, came every month and slowly drained Ram Gopal of everything he ever had...including his dignity. They first mortgaged his land as part payment and then his home. He shifted the family to a single room. After all this, Ram Gopal was still left with debts he could never repay.

There was only one way out, he decided. Suicide!

"What is that beautiful aroma?" asked Brahma, sniffing deeply as he walked along the open fields with his friends.

"It's called fresh air." Amir too filled his lungs with large gulps of the unpolluted countryside air, immediately feeling rejuvenated and full of vigour.

The two, along with Rahul and Patrick, had come away from New Delhi for a short holiday. Rahul's family friends had invited them to stay at their farmhouse. They were twenty kilometres from the township of Khurja and were now out for a stroll in the countryside surrounded by natural beauty.

"Its late for lunch, so lets take the short cut through that cluster of trees," advised Bharat Singh, their host's son, urging the happy lot on.

"Cluster of trees?' It's more like Tarzan's homeland, I would say." Brahma complained as they entered the thicket.

"I really wouldn't mind if Tarzan, or even Zimbo, jumped down from one of these trees, as long as its not one of his hairy apes or..."

"*LOOK OUT, BHARAT!!*"

Next instant, something whizzed past above them and struck something directly over and behind them. They lunged forward in fright, almost tripping over each other, even as they heard a soft thud behind them. Before they could see what it was, another warning went off.

"MOVE AWAY!! IT'S A SAW-SCALED VIPER!!" said the same voice.

"*RUN!!*" screamed Bharat, pushing the others on. Brahma never ever needed a second warning. When someone shouted 'run', he always did just that, instantly. He was naturally the first one off the blocks this time too, as he raced off some distance away before even thinking of putting up the question, 'why?' He looked back and noticed that the others had run away too, though not as far as him.

Out from the woods appeared a young boy, a catapult dangling in his hands.

"Amol!" cried out Bharat, nervously taking another look at the ground behind them.

"It was a Saw-scaled viper. He was hanging from that branch just above you all and was about to strike. I think, I have stunned it with my catapult shot."

"Whew!! But where has he gone?"

As the city boys looked on, Bharat and Amol picked up a large stick each and approached the spot they had run away from. And then they all saw it. Just two feet long the deadly snake looked harmless, as it lay unmoving within the tall grass.

"Careful," warned Bharat circling the snake. "It may be pretending. One scratch from its fangs and it's the end for the victim."

He brought his stick heavily down on the snake and suddenly it sprang to life. Another blow on its head even as it lunged forward to attack Bharat, and it writhed and squirmed in pain. A dozen further blows from both the boys and it lay still… dead.

"God!!" exclaimed Patrick almost white with fear. "Give me my New Delhi any day, pollution and all."

Bharat lifted the reptile on the stick and tossed it into the bushes. "These things happen frequently here, though this is just the second time in my life that I've seen a Saw-scaled viper. They are amongst the most poisonous snakes in India along with the King Cobra."

"Wow! But surely there are antidotes available, to act against the poison."

"There are, but not against all snake bites. The closest place for an antidote for this snakebite will probably be a hospital in New Delhi. The poison can kill a man in minutes so victims from these parts rarely survive."

"Do you know, more than 20,000 Indians get killed every year from snake bites. This snake and the King Cobra account for most of them," put in Amol casually.

Rahul, Patrick and Amir together gulped hard.

"We must thank this boy for saving us," said Rahul. Then turning towards Brahma he called out aloud, "Brahma! You can come back now. The snake is dead."

"No thanks. I feel safer here." By now Brahma had moved a good hundred meters away.

"There may be another one there!" warned Amir.

Next instant, Brahma was back with the group, a very alert pair of eyes keeping a constant watch around him. Then he looked sheepishly at the others and meekly said, "you know how I loathe these creatures."

"Forget about that incident. I want you lot to meet our saviour, Amol Ram Gopal. He lives close by and is a good friend of mine." Bharat introduced the boy individually to the four very grateful city boys.

The six boys walked homeward together, the city boys excitedly chatting of the close shave they had just experienced.

Amol hardly spoke a word, as his mind was more on the problems back home.

"Your friend is very quiet," observed Rahul, showing concern.

"Er...ahem...its a personal matter, and I'm not sure I am privileged to discuss it."

"It's alright, Bharat," stepped in Amol. "I don't mind if you tell them."

The casual chat stopped as Bharat explained the difficulties Amol's family was going through. "And finally the situation has become so grim that the moneylender has confiscated their land and even their home. Now, if Amol's father cannot pay up the dues by the end of this month, the moneylender has threatened to throw Amol and his family out of the single room too. They will probably have to live on the streets of the town very soon. The shame of the matter is that the moneylender's son, Raju, is Amol's best friend."

"Gosh! How terrible!" was the reaction from the four.

"Isn't there anything that can be done?" asked Amir who came from a poor family During his childhood he had known what it was like to go to bed at night on an empty stomach.

"My father has done all he could. He has worked for twenty hours a day, but the dues have kept mounting. And now we are all worried about him."

"Him only? Why?"

There was an uncomfortable silence as the boys trudged on, their speed reduced to a slow, reluctant walk.

Bharat cleared his throat for the umpteenth time and explained, "er…ahem…this year already two farmers from this village have committed suicide due to their unmanageable debts. Amol is worried his father may be driven to the same fate very soon."

They all stopped walking as though a wall had suddenly loomed up in front of them. Not a word was exchanged as the city boys silently sympathised their new friend. Such hardship to bear for such young shoulders.

The walk continued in studied silence.

"I heard there are bank loans available for small farmers," said Brahma suddenly. "Why don't they take a loan from a local bank?"

"Quite so. Most banks are inclined to give loans to small farmers," confirmed Bharat. "But there are certain other problems. The farmers being illiterate, and perhaps even timid, they are hesitant to approach banks who they believe work only in English. There are some farmers who don't even know of such facilities. And then, there are the moneylenders who feed them with false information and coax them instead to deal with them only, the traditional way. The difference being the moneylenders charge more than ten times the interest the banks charge.

"Why can't Amol's father take a bank loan and pay up this moneylender?"

"We tried to do just that when we found out about their problem," informed Bharat. "But bank loans can be had only against the mortgage of land or building. As Amol's father had already mortgaged his land and house to the moneylender, the banks naturally refused the loan."

"What a shamble. But there must be something we can do about it." Amir was all concentration as he focused on the problem. He refused to accept the fact that a greedy and unscrupulous man could herd a family out of their own home, and nobody could do anything about it.

"You know what? I think I may have the solution." Everyone turned to Rahul with such surprise as though he had just said, 'I know the man on the moon'.

"I was waiting for you all day," complained Raju, the moneylender's favourite son. He was of the same age as Amol.

"I was busy, but here I am now. So let's play." Amol had brought his friend out as per his city friend's plan, and the two were walking towards a particular spot selected by the boys. He did not much care for their idea, and was not even confident of it working successfully, but he knew 'a drowning man would clutch even at a straw to save himself'.

"So let's play here."

"No, a little ahead. I've seen a new spot where no one will disturb us." Hope the boys don't hurt him, thought Amol worriedly, looking fondly at the unsuspecting Raju.

They reached the selected spot, about half a kilometre away from both the boys' homes. Amol looked around casually, but couldn't see the city boys. Good, they were well hidden.

"What do we play?" Raju looked unsure of Amol's plans, but trusted him.

"Let's play wrestling."

"Oh no, that's too rough. Let's play…"

"Come on we are boys, and we are supposed to be rough and tough." Amol mocked and laughed and jumped on Raju, bringing him down. Soon the two were on the ground happily pitching each one's strength against the others. A while later, Amol was on top, pushing Raju's head down hard against the ground. At the same time he gave a signal.

First move was Amir's. With a homemade device of two pins attached to a matchstick an inch apart, he sneaked in close to the wrestling boys unnoticed. Suddenly, he jabbed his 'two-pin-weapon' lightly at the back of Raju's thigh. Raju let out a yell and tried jumping up, but Amol held him down with all his might, till Amir disappeared behind the trees again.

Next moment, the peaceful spot was a scene of commotion. From seemingly out of nowhere the other boys jumped out and started screaming 'SNAKE! SNAKE!" At the same time a few sticks banged heavily on the ground.

"Get off me!!" yelled Raju, shrugging off Amol from him. In amazement he saw a few boys mercilessly beating something on the ground. Shakily he got up and walked towards them holding his leg where he had felt the sting. In the midst of the excited boys he saw a dead and battered snake. It was a deadly Saw-scaled viper.

"What happened to you?" asked Amol with faked concern. Why are you holding your leg?

"I...I...think...I got stung by...something..." Raju nervously craned his neck to examine the back of his leg. "Oh my God! Th...there are...two tiny drops of blood as though...as though...I've been bitten by a snake!"

"Let me see," Amol examined the wound closely. The two tiny holes certainly did look like snakebite. Hats off to these boys. It was a real neat job, and couldn't have hurt Raju much either.

"It is a snake bite!" he jumped back, trying to look terrified "It...it...must be...the Saw-Scaled-Viper. Quick, we must get him to the doctor. You boys wait here, I'll inform his father."

Saying that, he ran off towards Raju's house.

"Good," thought Rahul with a half smile. "First part of the charade over. Now, to twist the money-lender's arm."

Meanwhile, Patrick made Raju lie down on his stomach and massaged the area around the marks. "Don't worry, you will be alright soon." While massaging he also applied some paste made of black soot.

"What do you mean, 'don't worry'? Don't you know this snake can kill a person, unless an antidote is applied immediately?"

"AMOL!! AMOL!!"

A boy came running towards them. "Where's Amol? I have an important message for him." He said breathlessly.

"He has gone to fetch Raju's father." Bharat came forward nervously, half guessing the message. "What happened Chhotu?"

"His father was seen walking towards Nayatri Falls!"

"*OH NO!!*" Bharat saw the concerned faces of his city friends and explained. "Nayatri Falls is a very high water fall. The two farmers who committed suicide earlier, had both jumped off its steep slopes."

"Dear God!" Patrick realised the gravity of the situation. "Here we are so close to solving his problem, and he wants to..." He couldn't complete the sentence.

"We must stop him. We must..." Rahul was holding his head trying to figure out what they should do next.

"The falls are closer from here, though still about three kilometres away," informed Bharat excitedly. "Rahul you come with me. We can race to the falls and may be beat Amol's father to it. These three can take care of the money lender when Amol brings him."

"Yes, you go...and fast," said Patrick. "We'll take care of the situation here."

With that assurance, Bharat and Rahul charged off at full speed on their desperate mission...a mission that could prove to be a matter of life and death.

"*Where is he? Where is he?*" Bhanu Singh, the moneylender, cried woefully, leading the small team of well-wishers. Amol was with him too, his large innocent eyes darting about him, now scared of the dangerous game they were playing. Patrick and Brahma were nursing the boy while Amir was out of sight.

"Where are Rahul and Bharat?" he inquired of Patrick in a whisper, as Bhanu Singh ran and threw his arms around his son, Raju.

"They'll be here soon," whispered back Patrick, trying his best to look casual and not alarm Amol. There was no point, they had agreed upon, of informing Amol of his father's plight. It would only hamper his act in front of the moneylender. Which in turn, may jeopardise the only chance Amol and his family would have of resettling into normal life.

"Oh God! Dear God!! Why have you brought this curse on me?" Bhanu Singh was crying aloud, tears pouring down his distraught face. The boys knew they could never play such a cruel trick on anyone else. But this bloodsucker deserved it.

"Did you get a doctor?" Patrick pretended to help Bhanu Singh nurse the boy's wound. "I have bound a handkerchief tightly round his upper thigh so that the poison won't go easily into the rest of his body."

"Thank you, my friend," said a grateful Bhanu Singh. "Alas my boy is going to die as the village doctor did not have the venom or the antidote for a Saw -scaled viper's bite."

"We have the venoms of other snakes, but it is not going to help." Amol explained applying something from a small bottle on Raju's thigh.

The anxious looks of his father and the other villagers around him made Raju feel genuinely sick. Was he going to

die? Scared, he cried and held on tightly to his father. Patrick and Brahma felt disgustingly guilty at involving young Raju, but it was all for a good cause.

"My life!! All my wealth and land, for a few drops of the antidote!!" cried Bhanu Singh dramatically. "Anything God, anything! Just let my son get well."

"I don't want all your wealth, and I don't want your land!" a loud voice came out of the woods. *"But I can make your son well again!"*

"What?? Who said that?"

"I said that!" From behind the trees stepped out Amir. He had removed his shirt and trousers and had fully covered himself with a white cloth. His long hair was completely tousled and he carried a stout stick.

"A young fakir?" Bhanu Singh and the others were taken aback as Amir stood in front of them challengingly, eyes flaring wide. "Who are you? Where did you come from? I've never seen you before."

"Are you more interested in knowing me or saving the life of your son?" Amir asked furiously, banging his stick on the ground.

"Ca...can you save him?" Bhanu Singh was kneeling down hands folded.

"YOU DOUBT ME??"

"No *Babaji*, no! I can see, you have the power."

"What were you saying earlier, that you would give away all your wealth and all your land?"

Bhanu Singh immediately wilted and shakily answered, "er…yes…but…but…"

"I see you really don't care for your son's life. So be it!" With that Amir turned around and started walking back towards the trees.

"No wait!! *Babaji*, I'll give away anything you wish. Just give me back my son."

"I already told you I want nothing from you. Just give back what you have taken from my friend Ram Gopal, and I'll cure your son."

"Er…who? What?"

"Ram Gopal is my family friend." Amir once again flared his eyes showing great anger. "And you have ruined him!!"

"No *Babaji*, no. I've just tried to help him and gave him a loan."

"I know all about your loans! I now ask you to return his land and his home that you have confiscated. And forget about your loan, which he has already repaid many times over, with interest. DO YOU HEAR ME??"

"Yes *Babaji*, yes." Bhanu Singh did some quick mental calculations and came up with a figure that he would give up for his son's life.

"Well do you agree, or should I leave?" Amir asked haughtily, now finding the role he was playing easy to perform.

"I agree! I agree," said Bhanu Singh quickly.

"In front of all these villagers say aloud that you will return all papers pertaining to Ram Gopal's land-deed and his house, and that Ram Gopal hereafter owes you nothing."

Bhanu Singh gulped hard, but repeated what Amir said. He quickly added, "but only if you cure my son".

"Agreed!" said Amir, nobly.

He next took out a small bottle of tap water and walked up to Raju.

"Everyone move away from the boy!" he demanded. "For the next few minutes only I will attend to him."

Rahul and Bharat ran over two kilometres and were on the point of collapsing.

"Still no sign of Ram Gopal!" panted Rahul, struggling to catch his breath. "Are we…too late?"

"Keep running… and praying. We do not know the lead he has on us. The waterfall is not far now."

Soon, Rahul could hear a faint rumbling sound and a little later the deafening roar of the waterfall. The loud fearsome sound and the critical mission that they were on scared him as never before.

"Where could…he be?" Rahul was holding his sides and bending over in exhaustion as their tearing run came to an end. The waterfall was quite narrow but very, very high. "I can't…see anyone. May be he is still on his way. May be he changed his…"

"THERE HE IS!!"

Rahul looked at the direction in which Bharat's finger was pointing. On the other side of the falls, sitting on the edge of a large rock that was jutting out precariously over the falls, was the saddest man he had ever seen. It seemed he was carrying the burden of the entire world on his back. His head was hanging low on his chest and he seemed to be mumbling something. Praying is what Rahul guessed.

"*RAM CHACHA!!* Your troubles are over!" shouted Bharat. But there was no response from the man across the falls.

"He cannot hear you over the roar of the falls. Let's shout together."

"**RAM CHACHA!!**" The two friends hollered with all their might but Ram Chacha looked on downwards, the speed of his fervent prayer seemingly getting more intense.

"How did he get across? And why?"

"A little further up the stream there are rocks that one can use, to cross over. And the reason he is on the other side is perhaps that protruding rock. It has a direct plunge onto the rocks below. It leaves no chance for survival."

"So let's quickly go upstream and cross over…*Oh no!!* He is…standing up…"

"He's moving closer to the edge! What do we do?"

"*RAM CHACHA!! RAM CHACHA!!*" the two desperately screamed, but yet to no avail. They saw Ram Chacha inch still further with his toes now outside the edge and fearfully peering down the steep cliff.

"Bharat you run to the spot where the rocks are, and cross over! I'll try to distract him somehow."

Bharat sprinted off without a word.

Rahul desperately yelled, jumping up and down and waving his arms in all directions, hoping to catch Ram Gopal's eye. And then he saw Ram Gopal had even shut his eyes as the tempo of his prayers reached the highest point.

Rahul threw a quick glance upstream. Bharat still hadn't reached the point where he could cross over. He will surely be too late. Just then a desperate idea struck him.

He picked up a stone the size of his fist. The stream was about fifty meters wide and as a decent cricketer, he could throw a ball much further than that. He saw the serene look on Ram Gopal's face and knew he was about to jump. He took aim, prayed to God to help him hit his target and flung the stone with all his might.

"That's it! You can stand up now, boy," declared Amir, dramatically spreading his arms and raising them slowly above his head, for a better effect.

Raju stood up shakily and saw the small crowd cheer as though they had just witnessed a miracle.

"Raju? God be praised, you look all right," Bhanu Singh stood blinking in disbelief. "Even the patch around the bite has gone."

Of course, he was not to know that it took just plain water to remove the dark patch. Reciting unheard of mantras Amir had rhythmically rubbed off the black soot, which was applied earlier.

"*Babaji*, you are truly great!" Bhanu Sigh was on his knees, holding Amir's legs. "Thank you, thank you…I don't know how to thank you fully."

"I've already told you how you should thank me. Now go home and return Ram Gopal's property papers back to him. And don't forget, he owes you nothing any longer."

Er…yes…but…"

"Any tricks and the curse will befall your son again!"

"No, no…no need for that. I'll do as you said."

With that the somewhat happy moneylender and his very puzzled son led the group back towards their house, leaving the boys behind.

Amol's eyes were dazzling with excitement and he laughed aloud with joy when they were alone. "I…still can't believe we did it. We actually fooled them all. But where are Bharat and Rahul? They missed all the fun."

Amir, Patrick and Brahma shuffled their feet uncomfortably and avoided looking at Amol. How does one break such news to one so little, they wondered. Finally, Amir found the strength and explained everything.

"WHAT?" It seemed Amol's legs had suddenly turned to rubber as he almost crumpled down to the ground. "But why didn't you tell me earlier? Why didn't you…oh I hate you all! You are not my friends."

Tears rolling down his face he ran clumsily towards the route Bharat and Rahul had taken. In his blind haste he stumbled repeatedly, till the city boys took hold of him. Initially he struggled against them, but finally ran along with them, refusing to even think of what might have become of his father.

When they reached the falls, drained out physically and emotionally, they were shocked at the sight that confronted them. Across the falls Amol's father was lying on the rocky ground, his face covered in blood. Rahul, the heavier of the two boys, was sitting on top of him while Bharat was holding his arms down. Ram Gopal seemed to be struggling silently while the two boys were hollering at him.

"Wh…what's going on?" stammered Amol, not believing his eyes. "Why are they…hurting my father?"

Patrick, Amir and Brahma together called out at the top of their voices and finally caught the attention of the boys across the falls. Rahul and Bharat gestured wildly and told them to go upstream and cross over to their side.

With shaky knees Amol at once started running upstream. He slowly understood what might have occurred. They all crossed over together holding each other's hands for support and ran back towards the struggling three.

As Amol ran forward and held his father tightly, Bharat and Rahul gently released Ram Gopal.

"Whew!" sighed Rahul, stretching his strained body. "A few more minutes and he would have shaken us off. He may be lean, but he is strong as an ox."

"What happened back there? Did our plan work against the money lender?" Bharat asked anxiously.

"Its all over, father, we are free again. We are free to live our lives without fear from the money lender." Amol was shaking his father by his shoulder; face wet with tears but beaming like a beacon.

"What are you talking about? And who are all these boys?"

"Friends, father. They are our true friends. I had prayed for an answer to our problems. They are the answer to my prayers. But where did you hurt yourself? You are still bleeding."

Apologetically, Rahul cleared his throat and confessed. "It was the only way I could stop him from jumping. My strong throw forced him to stumble backward. If the stone had hit him lightly he would have instead fallen forward, over the cliff.

Next day, with the deeds of his property firmly in his hands and a large bandage on his head, Ram Gopal entered the local branch of State Bank of India along with Bharat's father. An hour later, they walked out again, where the boys were waiting with baited breath.

"*I have it!*" shouted Ram Gopal, openly showing his happiness. "I have the loan I wanted, against the mortgage of my land."

Later, the four friends were back in the bus heading homeward to Delhi.

"Back to civilisation and a way of life we understand," said Brahma with a sigh of relief. "I can tell you guys that it will take more than clean air to coax me to return to the land of deadly snakes."

"Yes, that was real dangerous," Patrick agreed. "But what got me more was our treatment to the money lender. Don't you think it was terrible of us to play such a nasty trick on him?"

The others thought for a moment and in unison replied, "NAAAAH!!"

❑❑❑

3

The Legacy of Raghunathan

Raghunathan decided he wouldn't let that happen. If they wanted his money, they will have to work for it and use their unexercised brains.

Raghunathan was getting old and he knew his end was near. He had known a very successful and rewarding life, first as a farmer and then as a trader. Basically a happy and contented person, he also was a very wealthy man. But there was one aspect of his life that he was not satisfied with...the unremarkable spirit of his two idling sons.

Both the sons were in their forties, and together with their families lived with Raghunathan in his big house, on the outskirts of Pudukkottai. Raghunathan basically loved them, but detested their way of life. They were a pair of the laziest, most quarrelsome and ignorant men around. For years, Raghunathan's farmland had remained unattended. While he

concentrated on trading and accumulating wealth, his unenterprising sons, to whom he had entrusted the farming business, allowed the land to go to waste. Preferring to laze around the whole day they actually lived off the earnings of their father. Worse, the brothers and their families never got along well with each other either and were always arguing at any given opportunity. And now, Raghunathan knew, both the families were just waiting for him to die and enjoy his wealth. This is what Raghunathan regretted most in his life.

Two months later, Ragunathan died. It was July 1999.

After all the funeral formalities were over the two sons, Ramanath and Somanath, set about finding out what they had inherited. They found little or no money in their father's room. They searched for documents in case he had invested in companies or had bought assets. There were none. They looked for his bank accounts, but when they saw the balance in the passbook, their hearts broke. There was just the minimum balance and a huge amount of fifteen lakhs was withdrawn just a couple of months ago.

Frantically, they ransacked the house thinking he may have hidden his wealth in some secret compartment within the walls or even underground. But the search was in vain.

Just when they thought all was lost and they would all soon be penniless, a letter came from a solicitor's office in Madras. It said that shortly before he died, Raghunathan had left a will, to be executed by their firm. The letter was a summons for the two sons to go to Madras and receive the will.

Excited that their father had not abandoned them after all, the two sons immediately set off for Madras.

"The will states that his entire estate, that is, his land and his wealth, is to be passed on to you both in two stages," began the stern looking solicitor. "The first part, the land, he passes on to you with immediate effect."

The brothers exchanged happy looks. They knew that the land itself would fetch a handsome price and their immediate financial problem would be solved as soon as they managed to sell it.

"This land is never to be sold," continued the bespectacled solicitor, almost reading their minds. "The will says, the land is to be tilled by you both for the next five years. The earnings from it will be more than sufficient to look after you and your families."

"WHAT!!" both the brothers exclaimed simultaneously. "But we are not farmers. We…we…would not know what to do."

"Then learn it," said the elderly solicitor unemotionally. "There is more to it. Your first year's production must yield these many tonnes of food grain." He showed them the figure.

"No way!! This kind of target will mean a lot of time."

"So start today. After the first year's production, which you will confirm to this office with the sales receipt, you will have to increase the production every year by at least ten percent. Any year you fail in meeting the target you will lose all rights to his estates. The land and the entire accumulated wealth will be passed on to a charitable institution."

The brothers gaped at each other in disbelief. They had not expected such a harsh decision from their father.

"But...what about the wealth? When do we get that?"

"After five years of conformity with the task given, you will be instructed about his wealth. And one more thing, you are not to sell either a single square foot of the land, or any item from the house during the five years. I have the full inventory of the items and we will check them upon completion of the period."

On returning home, the dejected brothers tried to find a loophole in the will and somehow squirm out of its limitations. But there were no such loopholes. Soon, they realised whatever money they possessed was fast disappearing too.

Begrudgingly, they laid their hands on farming tools and began tilling their land. The skin of their soft hands often tore but soon the hands toughened. Their backs strained with pain every night, but soon that same back could carry large loads. Where at first they couldn't work beyond a few minutes, they now worked for over twelve hours a day in the fields. And more importantly, they began working together. Peace had gently regained its position in the house and they lived happily together.

By the end of the first year, the brothers met their targeted production and satisfied the solicitor's office. Every year thereafter, they did achieve an increase in production by over ten percent. The families now lived a comfortable life. The thought of a pot of gold at the end of the rainbow, here at the end of five years, inspired them further to struggle on.

Five years went by and the brothers became seasoned and successful farmers. They looked forward to the reward of their father's wealth. On the appointed day after the fifth year, they reached the solicitor's office and made their claim.

"Today I am happy and proud to pass on to you the paper that will instruct you where your father's wealth is," congratulated the old solicitor with the faintest of smiles, handing over to them a sealed envelope.

With trembling hands the brothers tore open the envelope and took out a slip of paper. They read it, failed to understand it, and re-read it several times further.

"It's...a kind of...a cryptic poem, or something like that," complained Ramanath. "But where is his wealth?"

"That's all I have to give you, gentleman." The unfriendly solicitor stood up, indicating the meeting was over. "I believe the message in the poem will guide you to his wealth. Don't worry, he has given you another year to solve the riddle, failing which the entire amount will be donated to a charitable institution he has chosen. Though the land now is yours to hold. You have earned it."

The brothers went back home and spent all their time and energy in breaking the code to the cryptic riddle. Their wives and children tried helping but none could understand it. Soon frustrations crept in, quarrels sprang up and the family was almost tearing itself apart. The farm was again neglected, though not abandoned, and it seemed it was just a matter of time before the two brothers would sell the farm and separate. All the work put in by them together was about to go to waste. Soon, the stipulated time for finding the solution to the riddle was coming to a close. Just two months remained.

When Rishi heard the story from his friend Sonu, son of Somnath (the younger son of Raghunathan), he found it difficult to express how he felt...sad at the plight of his friend's family, or admiration for Raghunathan's plot to make his sons work.

"Whereas my grandfather wanted the family to stay together and think together, it has resulted in dividing us." Sonu completed his narration miserably.

"What a puzzle Raghunathan must have worded that none of you could decipher it," observed Rishi with awe.

"I have read it several times too, but could not make head or tail of it. And we don't want to show it to any expert or anyone outside our family, for fear of losing the wealth to them."

"Well you don't have much time left as I see it. In any case, you will lose the entire amount to some charitable institution if you don't come up with the solution soon."

"I don't see what we can do about it, but an outsider will just not be acceptable."

"Maybe breaking the code requires an outsider...may be it has a simple translation that has bypassed the eyes of your close-knit family who may be thinking, in a kind of, single channel only."

"But we have tried everything, and interpreted each word in a different way, and even tried reading between lines to find an inner meaning. Everything!"

"Can you make a copy…for me?"

"WHAT? How can I? It's a family secret."

"I know, but if it can save your family from self-destruction I think it's worth…"

"But you are just a boy too. What can you do what the grown-ups have failed to do?"

"That's just my point. The clue to the puzzle may be more easily identified by our simple and clear minds, than those with biased and busy minds."

"I don't know, I have tried it too, and so have my cousins. But about making a copy, my father would be furious if I dared. And if my uncle came to know of it he might even kill me. He is so hot tempered…"

Next day at school, a quivering Sonu did bring a copy of the cryptic message.

"I've scribbled the text here…but please, please make sure no one else gets to see it." With a great show of secrecy Sonu let Rishi have a quick peek at the puzzle before he quickly slipped it back into his pocket.

After school, when they had found a secluded spot in the school field Rishi got to read the contents of the cryptic message fully. It read:

At the Seat of Learning

Neglected yet yearning

Lies the route to the Pot of Gold

Which when discovered, can never be sold.

Is it at the School of the Saint?

Or the College without a Taint?

Could it be at the Ashram of the Enlightened

Or the Academy for the Culturally Inclined.

The answer lies in the Strength of the Arms

By the greatness of 'Om',

In the Fragrance of the Hard Rose

In the humbleness of your Home.

"We did do a lot of thinking and have narrowed down the search to St Joseph's School for 'School of the Saint'; Institute of Pure Science for 'College without a Taint'; taking 'pure' to mean 'untainted'. Ram Krishna Mission we thought must be the 'The Ashram of the Enlightened'. The fourth clue, 'Academy for the Culturally Inclined', we are still not sure but it could be the Academy for Music."

Rishi appreciated the wisdom in their solutions.

"We all have even visited the places, but moved around aimlessly as we just didn't know where to look and what to look for. Is it a box of money and jewellery, or a file of documents, like shares and deposit certificates?

Thereafter, we also figured out that 'Strength of Arms' should mean something heavy to be moved. 'By the Greatness of Om' again detracted us as this could mean a Mandir or something religious again. 'Hardness of Rose' totally defeated us, but 'Humbleness of Home' may be a decoy to mislead us as there was nothing in the house."

Rishi didn't reply. He wanted time for the riddle. Not that he was confident of cracking it, but to try and make some sense out of it. At home, he went through it a hundred times to see if there was a hidden clue somewhere. He fiddled with the words and letters, rearranging them in different sequences. He tried to number the letters to see if some new light could be thrown on the enigma. By midnight he had to give up. He concluded that the guesses Sonu's family had come up with were by far the best ones.

But the four places they had short-listed were huge places. If you do not know what you are looking for, and exactly where, it would be futile to go about it blindly.

"Can I come over to your house this evening?" Rishi asked Sonu when they met at school next day.

"What for?"

"I myself don't know. May be just to get a feel of the place...and your family."

"Nobody is in any mood to entertain you, believe me. You will feel unwelcome."

"I don't mind."

Sonu hadn't exaggerated the foul mood within his family. Frowns, scowls, short tempers and insults were the flavour of the season. Nobody welcomed Rishi; instead they made it clear they didn't care much for new faces around the house.

"Sorry, but I did warn you, and you still haven't met my uncle," apologised Sonu.

"That's okay, I really don't mind. But I must say your family is pretty big."

"There are eleven of us living here…that too with two of our grandfather's rooms out of bounds for us all. As per his will his two rooms were to be left alone."

"That's definitely very cramped, but does that mean no one has been to those two rooms in years?"

"I know what you are getting at. But those rooms were the first that the family searched. Every drawer of every cupboard, as every inch of those rooms, was carefully scrutinised. Nothing. Now we just go in there once a week to keep it clean."

Rishi moved about the house pretending to play with Sonu. A few insults were hurled at him indiscriminately, but he kept flashing his disarming smile. At the same time his eyes were peeled for any hint or clue, any abnormality that he could link to the riddle. But he too drew a blank. However, a faint hunch kept telling him that the house might reveal the secret to the mystery. Something that the residents had missed as it had been in front of their eyes for years. But by late evening, he too was convinced the answer lay elsewhere. Dejectedly, he left the house with Sonu.

"What about your grandfather's rooms? Can I see them?" He asked suddenly in the middle of the road.

"Of course not! We keep them under lock and key. In any case it's all so dirty there now that you cannot differentiate between the wooden and the metal furniture."

"Can we not make some excuse, like cleaning the place for... free and..."

"No. That would be too messy. In any case the dirt on the furniture would be impossible to remove without soap and water."

"I got it! Tomorrow is Sunday. Tell them I have a special solution that cleans old wooden furniture very well. Which as a matter of fact, I do have. My cousin brought it from abroad and it cleans all grime and dirt like no other cleaner."

"But what do you expect to find there?"

"I told you I don't know," cried out Rishi in exasperation. "I just could not make out anything of the cryptic message, so I thought a more direct approach might help. That's all."

"But, but...my uncle...he'll...he'll..."

Next morning after a grudging approval from Sonu's father, the boys set about cleaning old Raghunathan's rooms. They first tackled his bedroom. Scantily furnished, it had a large and high wooden bed, a wooden cupboard, a rocking chair and a few metal trunks.

They started with the bed. Removing the mattress and the pillows, they applied the solution all around. Almost magically the bed became spotlessly clean. All the grime and dirt of the past seven years came off easily, bringing out the original colour of the wood. Before putting back the old mattress they explored the woodwork of the bed, probing for hidden levers for secret compartments. Finding nothing, they poked and pounded at the mattress and pillows for anything that was not soft cotton. Nothing.

They next tackled the wardrobe. Besides a few clothes it was full of different mementoes and souvenirs. Here Rishi felt they could pick up a clue. "Look for anything that connects with any of the words in the riddle…it may be a photograph or a picture or may even be just a worded message."

Bringing out all its contents they first searched the wardrobe itself. Here the possibilities of a hidden compartment were immense too and so Rishi was set to spend a lot of time investigating it. He started by feeling the back panel from top to bottom. As he pushed the section between the second and third shelf, he felt it move by half an inch. Excited they prodded and pulled at it.

A sudden shout made them both jump out of their skins.

"*What are you two doing?* And who is this?"

They swung round to face the wrath of Ramanath, Raghunathan's elder son. He stood at the doorway, a stick in his hand and the foulest of frowns on his face.

"Th…this is my friend, Rishi," stammered an absolutely petrified Sonu. "Father gave us permission to clean these rooms with a special cleaner my friend has."

Ramanath considered this piece of information in silent anger.

"Who asked you to empty the cupboard?" he demanded looking at Rishi suspiciously. "*Put everything back inside immediately!*"

Quickly the boys replaced all the items in the cupboard, under the watchful eye of Sonu's uncle. When they had finished, he stepped forward and locked the cupboard with a large key.

"Clean only the outer surface, and don't touch anything else." With a clear warning hanging heavily in the room he strode away.

"Damn it!" exclaimed Rishi. "I am sure we would have found something in there...something that would have helped in solving the cryptic message. Even the trunks above the wardrobe look great possibilities, but they too are locked.

Dispirited they spent little time in the room. "We will try that wardrobe and the trunks some other day, when no one's around," comforted Rishi.

"Another day? You are forgetting we just have less than two months in hand. By then we have to submit the solution to the riddle."

Rishi regretted the stand the two brothers had taken. Neither would allow an expert code cracker to try and decode the message nor let anybody else help them.

"Let's try the second room without upsetting any furniture," suggested Rishi.

The first piece of furniture to catch Rishi's eyes was the decorative bookcase. The other items in the room included a simple writing table with a chair, a large settee and an umbrella holder that housed two overused walking sticks.

"Your grandfather seems to have been a scholar?" he remarked admiring the bookcase, which was packed with a variety of books.

"No, he was not a scholar, but he was a great reader and has collected books on almost every subject. He was particularly fond of subjects like carpentry and gardening. He also read extensively on subjects like marketing and management and also biographies and history. There are even some children's books."

"May be within these books there is a key to his message," pondered Rishi aloud. "But we don't have the time to go through so many books, but we can study the titles of each book and hope there is something to lead us to the riddle."

The two got down to studying the titles and even the synopsis, of the scores of books. Two hours later the weary boys gave up, not finding a single book that aroused their curiosity.

"What now? I think we'd better pack up, it's past your time to return home." said Sonu wearily.

"But we must clean the furniture here. That's what we came here for didn't we? You handle the book case, I'll clean the table and the chair."

Rishi cleaned the table first and was surprised as the almost black colour vanished and a deep brownish-red colour materialised. "Wow! This table today would surely fetch a good price," he observed with wonder. "It's made of rose wood. You know, a coat of varnish and this wood would become glowing red. Just look at those natural grains."

"Hmmm..." Sonu was not interested in being educated on the upkeep of wooden furniture.

Rishi next worked on the chair. That too was obviously made of rose wood, as the layers of grime was washed away and a beautiful shade emerged. Even as Rishi admired the wood, he found a design, ingrained on the backrest of the chair. Speechless with his discovery, he took a few steps backwards. For a few minutes all he could do was look on, while his mind raced through the words of the riddle.

"What's wrong with you?" asked Sonu. "You look as though you have seen a ghost."

Rishi simply pointed at the backrest of the chair.

"What?" Sonu complained irritably and walked up to the front of the chair. He peered closely at what Rishi was pointing.

Sonu's blank look annoyed Rishi. "Can't you see the sign?"

Sonu moved his head to look from another angle and immediately spotted it. "Oh yeah! It's very faint, but it is the sign of Om...and naturally made too. That's nice, but what shook you up so much?"

"Don't you see it, you oaf? Don't you see it at all?" exclaimed Rishi excitedly, unable to contain his delight. "It's all in here! The answer to Raghunathan's riddle is this chair!"

For a moment; Sonu was convinced that the strain of the riddle had finally got into Rishi too, as had happened to most of his family during the last one year. But Rishi interrupted his thoughts mid way.

"Allow me," he said, and explained all.

"At the Seat of Learning…

His chair in a way is a seat of learning, being the only chair in the study room.

Neglected yet yearning…

It was certainly neglected as it was hardly ever occupied by anyone, but Raghunathan himself.

Lies the Route to the Wealth…

So the chair itself is not wealth, but the way to it. But where in the chair lies the route?

The answer lies in the strength of the arms…

The arms of the chair obviously contains the route, may be even a map.

By the Greatness of Om…

Here the word 'by' must mean 'next to', hence, he meant next to the sign of Om.

In the Fragrance of the Hard Rose…

Here he is simply describing the chair as one made of Rose wood, which is one of the hardest varieties of wood available.

In the humbleness of your Home...

The chair as we all know is in your home. The entire second stanza was there as a decoy to simply misguide you."

Sonu heard him in total disbelief. Here indeed must lie the route to the wealth. There could be no doubt about it. He gave a yell of victory and ran to fetch his family.

The whole family gathered round the chair, staring at it as though it were a creature from outer space. In the middle was Sonu, beaming from ear to ear, and painstakingly explaining the relevance of the chair with every word of the riddle. When he finished, the family drew closer and lovingly touched the symbol of Om, as well as the arms of the chair.

"This is terrific, son," said Somanath, Sonu's father. "I am amazed how you hit upon the answer. But why is your friend still here?"

To avoid difficult explanations, the boys had pre-planned that Sonu should take credit for the discovery, as Rishi was not supposed to know of the riddle.

"It was Rishi who cleaned the chair and pointed out the sign, and then I put the riddle in perspective," explained Sonu. "I just couldn't ask him to leave after that. He deserves to be with us and celebrate our good fortune."

"But now he must leave!" stepped in Sonu's uncle, Ramanath. He certainly did not look pleased with Rishi's presence and told him off brusquely, "You may go downstairs and wait for us in the hall."

Amidst much protest from Sonu, Rishi left the room.

"Now to see if we can wriggle out the arm of the chair," said Somanath, gleefully fiddling with the arm.

A few twists and turns of the arm didn't help. Soon somebody brought some tools. A few screws were removed and the arms came free one after the other.

"Nothing!" cried out Somanath, almost in tears. "All the pieces are separated, but no sign of any note or map. Why did father make us go through all this trouble?"

"Wait a minute!" Ramanath examined one of the stumps of the chair's arm. "This looks like a filling used in wood work… yes it is." With a long screwdriver he scraped out the hardened clay and out came a rolled up piece of paper. A loud cheer went up and the family huddled together to read 'the route to the wealth'. Gone was the bitterness that had crept in between the two families.

Ramanath unrolled the paper to read the vital clue and instantly a frown settled upon his face.

"It's another damn riddle!" He cried out in exasperation. "What in heaven's name was father upto, putting us in such jeopardy?"

"But what does this riddle say?" asked Somnath half-heartedly. "Is it difficult too?"

The paper was spread out on the table, and all read it together.

Seekers of my Wealth

Will have to worm through fine,

For it is not with haste, but stealth

That they'll find their gold mine.

On Wings of Wisdom

You'll find my Kingdom,

Of that what I value most

But of which I cannot boast

In a leaf of my tree

You'll find, 'I came late to history',

Take it to the man in Madras

For now you'll no longer need to cut grass.

"God!" cried Sonu's father with anguish. "This all sounds gibberish to me. It'll probably take another long year to unravel this mystery. But we have just two months."

"It may sound gibberish to us," cut in Sonu. "but may be my friend can help."

Ramanathan turned sharply towards Sonu. "What do you mean? Are you hiding something from us?"

Sonu swallowed, hard but knew it was time to confess. He told them about Rishi's intelligence and his actual involvement in solving the first riddle. "I am sure he can help with this riddle too."

Ramanath and Somanath exchanged tentative glances. Somanath hesitatingly nodded his approval, but Ramanath stood firm. "I will allow him to come only if you agree that if this boy manipulates the message and we lose part of the money, then it will be from your share that will be lost. I will claim my full fifty percent."

On Sonu's insistence, Somanath agreed to the terms and allowed Rishi to come in. Rishi, upon joining the group, went through the riddle, as all waited expectantly, but could make no sense of it.

"No, it makes no sense to me either."

"*Bah!!* Just as I thought! You're making too much of this little boy. So where do we go from here? Back to cutting grass?"

"I'd suggest you make a few copies of this and distribute amongst each of us. We should spend at least one entire day individually on it and meet again tomorrow evening, and see if any of us has made a breakthrough." Saying this Rishi looked around to see how they reacted to his suggestion.

"You said 'we'!" countered Ramanath, still not liking the idea of an outsider to be involved in his family affairs. "How can we trust you with a copy? You may take it to an expert code breaker and..."

"Please uncle, you are talking to my friend!" said Sonu angrily stepping in. "If you don't trust him, then I too will have no part in this search." Sonu surprised himself and all around him with his sudden outburst.

"And if my son is out of this, so will the rest of my family." Came the support for Sonu from unexpected quarters…his father.

Finding himself alienated, Ramanath relented and allowed Rishi to have a copy too. Soon each was left with his or her copy, to try and pit their intelligence against the enigma.

It was indeed a riddle fit for a master code breaker, thought Rishi, turning for the umpteenth time in his bed. He had spent the rest of the day over the puzzle and now he couldn't even go to sleep with it tauntingly playing on his thoughts.

As a chance exercise he jumbled up each word, to see if individually they led somewhere. He tried to connect each word to some aspect of the house. He even went through the thesaurus to find other meanings of each word.

Next day after school, he walked with Sonu back to Raghunathan's house. All the occupants wore long faces and it didn't take a genius to know none had broken the code. They looked at him anxiously for some good news.

"The only connection I could make," began Rishi unconvincingly, "was the linkage of two words. One was 'worm' and the other 'leaf'. They can both refer to a book… *'worm'* as in 'bookworm', and *'leaf'* for a 'leaf of a book'. If this is a key then Raghunathan Thata could be referring to a book. But he is talking of a *'leaf of my tree'*. What this 'tree' is that he is referring to, could prove to be the vital link. Did he have any favourite tree? Did any one hear him talk of any one particular tree?"

There was silence as everyone tried to remember. After sometime Somanath said slowly, "I think he sometimes did refer to a tree. I'm sure he called it a tree, but it was not a tree."

"Then what was it?" asked Ramanath aggressively.

"I just can't remember." He kept looking up at the ceiling trying to make his brain work overtime.

"Let's go back to his rooms," suggested Sonu. "May be the answer, once more, is in there."

Upstairs, in Raghunathan's two rooms, the family and Rishi spread themselves out. "Go through every item, minutely. See if anything at all resembles a tree."

So they all searched...under the chair and above the wardrobe, inside the drawers of the table and behind the bed, until a stifled cry from Somanath caught everyone's attention. He was examining the bookcase and now was on his knees, scrutinising something at its base.

"What did you find?"

"It's the name of the maker of the bookcase. It is 'Gulmohor Pvt Ltd'! And...and...now I remember, father once called it 'my tree'. His library was his 'tree of knowledge'...and the different subjects were its 'branches'."

"I can't believe it! We have broken the code so quickly this time," said Ramanath with a tremble in his voice. "Now lets put the rest of the riddle in its perspective."

It didn't take them long to conclude that ***'they will have to worm through fine'*** would mean they will have to read every book in the bookcase. That they should do it ***'without haste, but stealth,' to find their goldmine. 'In a leaf of my tree'*** will be a page from one of the books'. They'll have to find one particular line that read as ***'I came late to history'***. The book with that line should be taken to the solicitor in Madras, and only then can they lay claim to their wealth.

"*Read all those books to find one line? Impossible!!*" growled Ramanath angrily. "There must be over a hundred books in there! I am sick of this entire exercise! You can do what you all want, I am going to..."

"Actually it is not impossible, if everyone contributed." All eyes turned to Rishi. "Till now your two families have tried to solve the riddles independently. I think Raghunathan Thata designed the entire sequence so that you all will work together on it, instead of quarrelling over it, as has been the case till now."

Sonu thought Ramanath was about to physically pick up Rishi and throw him out of the house. Ramanath's face had turned red, his nostrils flared and his lips twitched in a manner as never before. Sonu quickly stepped between Rishi and his uncle.

"How dare you speak so impertinently about my family?" hissed Ramanath with gritted teeth. He moved Sonu aside and towered over Rishi. "And how do *you* suggest we read all these hundred books? Spend our entire lives over it?"

"There seems to be about hundred and fifty books in that case," said Rishi calmly, unmoved by Ramanath's aggression. "And there are twelve of us, including me. If we distribute the books amongst us, each of us will have to go through about twelve books. With two months in hand, and if we devote at least five to six hours daily to read them, I am sure we can cover the lot."

The family stared back at him as though he had just spoken in Double Dutch.

"But Rishi," broke in Sonu, "none of us read anything, except maybe our school books."

"If you want that treasure, you'll have to change. This is the only way, as far as I can see." Rishi.

"There are all sorts of books in there which don't interest us at all."

"There is a way. Let us first categorise the books."

"Why?" Ramanath asked haughtily. He didn't like the idea of being ordered around by a young boy.

"That way we can all select the subjects...subject we like and understand, and read only those books." With much show of lethargy the family removed all the books and started sorting them. The summation of the inventory was:

15 books on Management

20 books on Marketing

19 books on Philosophy

12 books on Biography

6 books on Religion

6 books on Gardening

18 books on Farming

19 books of Children's Fiction

16 books of Adult Fiction

6 books on Indian History

6 books on the Freedom Movement

Total 143 books

The family consulted each other and they decided that the two brothers Ramanath and Somanath share the books on philosophy and religion. Sonu's senior cousins agreed to read the marketing and management books, while the junior cousins were to read Indian history, biographies and adult fiction. The two senior ladies wanted to read all about gardening and farming, while Sonu and his younger brother, along with Rishi had to tackle children's fiction.

The books now sorted, the family stood in a group, silent as though at a funeral. Obviously the load on their heads was heavier than what they would have liked.

"In two months time, I will not be able to read even one book," grumbled one of Sonu's cousins.

"You don't have to, you know," reminded Rishi curtly. "But you might as well kiss your inheritance good bye from now. As for me, I'll certainly do my bit and read my share of the books."

The family quietly dispersed, unsure of what they had got themselves into.

Next day after school, Rishi once again went to Sonu's house to check on any progress. He was aghast to see most of the books back in the bookcase, and the family shuffling around sullenly.

"What happened?"

"Everyone finds the task too demanding," explained Sonu. "They feel they'll never be able to read that much."

"You people are giving up without even trying?" Rishi asked exasperatedly. Don't you realise you might get lucky and hit upon that line in the first book itself?"

No answer. Rishi realised that to shake this family from its present inertness, something drastic needed to be done.

"So Raghunathan Thata was correct," he began, certain that his next words would result in either making them jump into action, or his own untimely demise. "You lot obviously like to live off other people's hard work. Well, so be it! As promised I'll do my part and go through all the books. If I am lucky and chance upon that line, I'll pass it on to you. You can lay claim to Raghunathan Thata's treasure without shedding a drop of sweat…as you've always done."

With that he strode out of the house, head held high, ready for the onrush of footsteps and his ultimate lynching. But no footsteps came and no shouts of protests could be heard. In fact, he didn't hear as much as a peep.

Rishi didn't meet Sonu for the next three days, not even at school. Worried he once again visited Sonu's house. From outside the complete hush that surrounded the house worried him even more. Some tragedy seemed to have befallen the house. He prayed that his short and sharp lecture was not responsible for whatever might have taken place.

He knocked softly on the door; hoping only Sonu would open it and warn him of any consequences. But it was Ramanath who opened the door. Rishi took a few quick steps backwards; ready to bolt at the first sign of aggression.

"Is Sonu at home?" he asked in a meek voice, keeping a good ten feet distance from Ramanath.

"Ssh…not so loud!" Ramanath admonished. "What do you want?" he asked sternly, hiding something in his left hand behind his back.

"Er…Sonu? Where's Sonu? I…haven't seen him at school for three days."

"He has been busy," came the curt reply. "I'll make sure he'll resume school tomorrow. Now off with you! We are all busy."

"Busy…with what?" Rishi dared to ask.

"*Reading!*" a sudden smile flashed on Ramanath's face as he brought his left hand forward. He was holding a book, a finger marking his present page. Rishi knew his parting shot had paid off.

Next day when they met, Sonu narrated what had happened.

"When you left that day after your scathing speech, the family was dumbstruck and no one spoke for sometime. Then

Ramanath Uncle, walked up to the bookcase, selected a book and without a word walked away to his room. Soon my father did the same, and later each one of us selected a book and started reading. You wanted us to read for five to six hours everyday, but can you believe no one has put in less than ten hours of solid reading per day? All other work has been put on hold. Things like cooking and farming has been almost neglected and given the bare minimum time. Even my cousins skipped school and college these last few days. At this rate, I am sure all the books will be read after all.

And so it was. On the fiftieth day, ten days before the ultimate D Day, Somanath jumped up from his bed with his current book and hollered, *'EUREKA!!'* so loudly that all of Pudukkottai must have heard him.

"Its here!! I've found the line!!" he gushed and called out to his family. "Here, on page 23 of 'The Discovery of India', by Pandit Jawaharlal Nehru, are the words 'I came late to history'. He wrote this book while in prison in Ahmednagar Fort in 1944, during his struggle against the British rule. He also makes a strange comment here. He says here that he always considered his present situation somehow connected to the past, and that once more soon, he would be part of history again."

The very next day, the two brothers once again visited the solicitor's office in Madras, to lay claim to the legacy left by their father.

"Bravo! Bravo! Bravo!" the stern solicitor uncharacteristically exclaimed with a very large smile, upon being presented the solution to the riddle. Reaching out to shake the hands of the two brothers he continued, "Very frankly friends, I didn't expect you to reach this far. How did you do it?"

"As frankly, Sir, we wouldn't have reached this far without the initiative of a boy," confessed Ramanath, now seemingly a changed man.

"Good, good, good. Now its time for your rewards." With that he went to a safe and returned with yet another sealed envelope. "This is it. You can now open it and enjoy the fruits of your labour."

Ramanath tore open the envelope and hastened to read the contents. Puzzled, he read it again and then read it a third time. Then he passed it on to Somanath. And as he saw Somanath read the contents with a puzzled expression, he burst out laughing. Somanath too read it twice and slowly smiled, and then joined his brother in a hearty laugh.

"What a wily old man our father was," cried Ramanath still heaving with laughter.

"Does it say where he has hidden the wealth?" asked the solicitor, appearing to be as interested in the outcome of this case as the two brothers.

"Read it for yourself," offered Somanath passing on the letter to him.

Intrigued, the solicitor read:

My dear sons,

I must have caused you a great deal of labour and tension. But if you have reached thus far as to read this, then my last wish has been fulfilled.

When I left you, both of you, and your families, were lazy, physically and mentally, and all of you often quarrelled and were selfish in your thoughts.

Now I know your hands and bodies are strong having worked on the fields, your heart and soul have cleansed as you must have worked as one family to solve the riddle, and your mind is now active and alive after having gone through all those books.

This is my only legacy for you and your families. Possessing these qualities you will never need anything more, ever."

Your father, Raghunathan.

The solicitor too had to read the contents a few times before he asked, "but what about the wealth you were expecting?"

"Obviously there is none." Ramanath said, getting up.

"But what about the fifteen lakhs he had withdrawn from the bank before he passed away? Where is that money?" asked Somanath, not willing to give up so easily.

"Fifteen lakhs you say?" the solicitor went back to the safe and returned with a receipt. "Through our office he made a donation of fifteen lakhs to the Rural Library Fund, as you say, about two months before his demise."

"Why didn't you tell us this before?"

"You never asked. Anyway, we were sure there was a larger amount kept aside for you."

When Sonu informed Rishi of the anticlimax trip to Madras, he too marvelled at the true value of Raghunathan's Legacy. Even in death he had actually guided his son's families, for there is no money on earth worth A *Healthy Body, A Sound Mind and A Good Soul.*

❑❑❑

4

Andrew and Anjali

The icy cold wind blew incessantly from the north. The skies were mainly clear with a few high clouds, and a just-risen sun peeped now and then from behind them, as though wondering if it was time for it to emerge completely and warm the earth. But obviously its instructions were otherwise. It quickly hid behind another cloud and allowed winter to take its course.

Me? It didn't make any difference really. My fur coat amply protected me. And my companion, Trixy, was too busy, talking non-stop, to worry about anything else.

"And can you imagine", she was saying with a quick glance towards me, "she actually bit her master's ankle!"

I was imagining, but not a wee bit about her friend's indulgences. I was imagining the sumptuous breakfast that I had missed, thanks to Trixy's idea of an early morning walk.

I was imagining the blissful sleep my friend Raja, the pariah, must still be enjoying.

Oho! I forgot to introduce myself. I am Cocktail or 'Cocky' for short. I believe I got the name from my mixed-breed origin, and I live with the Pradhan family in Darjeeling.

"Cocky, you haven't been listening to a word I am saying!" Trixy's sudden accusation shook me out of my thoughts.

"I am, I am listening to you," I said automatically. We were now walking on the farther side of our favourite stretch, the one-mile circle around Chowrasta. The birds were busy with their morning chores, Trixy's monotonous drawl continued and I was about to drift mentally once more when I heard a voice alien to these heavenly surroundings. Someone was downright angry and almost scolding in a controlled voice, as though afraid someone may be listening. But in these parts sound travels far, and yes, there are always listeners.

"I've told you earlier, and I am telling you again! *Stay away from that boy!!*" reprimanded a strong voice.

It stopped us both in our tracks. There was no one else on the road and my inquisitive companion instantly decided it was her moral duty to locate the source of the disturbance. She briskly moved to the edge of the road and scanned the huge valley below.

"That's Shekharbabu and his daughter, Anjali," she reported back dutifully. "You know she is the one I have been telling you about these last few days."

First time, I thought, I heard that name. I dared not ask when and what she had talked to me about her.

"Hmmm...just as I thought. Shekharbabu is lecturing her about Andrew," interpreted Trixy.

"Andrew?" I had found a nice sunny spot and was glad to take a break from the enforced walk.

"Yes...Andrew Budd...remember I had told you about him?"

"Uh...yeah, so what about him?"

"You never listen when I talk to you, do you?" she asked hotly, jerking me to attention. "He wants to marry Anjali, but the parents on both sides are against the match. *Now* do you remember?"

"Yeah, yeah, yeah...of course I remember," I replied quickly. "But why?"

"What 'but why'?"

"Why won't the parents let them get married?" repeated I.

"Good heavens!" she cried out in exasperation. "You must be the...sshhh...Anjali is saying something". She quickly returned to her post by the edge.

Anjali's voice was low so Trixy's ears went as high as they could, straining to catch even a whisper.

"But father, we love each other. We don't care what religion the other belongs to."

"Well we care!" The father thundered aloud making Trixy drop her ears down low. "We come from a very orthodox Hindu family and never in our history has any one married outside our caste!"

A stifled sniff and Trixy's ears jumped up again and her head twisted on her neck so that the ears were positioned correctly. I admired her radar-like response to every sound.

"You are never going to see that boy again, and that's final," came the stern warning from the father.

And that was the final word, as both walked away in silence. Disappointed, Trixy came back to me with a drooping head. "Isn't it sad? Thank God we don't have things like 'religion' in our world."

I had no clue as to what she was talking about so I gave a polite nod in the affirmative.

"I mean there is God, and we are all His creatures. That's the way we all see…why can't they?"

A sermon this early in the morning was not my cup of tea. "I am hungry," I said and headed back home.

Two days went by peacefully. On the third day, I was enjoying a particularly juicy bone with Raja, when Trixy came running.

"Guess what?" she gushed excitedly. "Anjali is getting married next week!"

"Yipee," I said under my breadth and concentrated on my juicy bone.

"Not to Andrew, you greedy fool," she countered angrily, nipping me on my shoulder. "Her father is forcing her to marry someone from their own caste. Someone she doesn't even love."

Having forced her attention on me, and having humiliated me in front of my friend by calling me names and nipping me, I had to put aside my juicy bone and confront her. "Listen, neither am I going to be the priest at their wedding, nor a guest. So why should I be interested in this stupid piece of news?"

Stung, she upped her nose, for which she was famous, turned on her toes like a ballerina and strutted off without a word.

My victory! There will definitely be trouble from Trixy later, I was sure, but right now I was on a high. Grinning I turned to Raja, "that put her in her place, didn't it?" I knew Raja hated Trixy and her upper class ways (just as much as Trixy hated Raja and his rough manners), and this rebuff should get a nod of approval from him.

"Uh-huh," he said, trying not to show too much interest. "But she did call you a 'greedy fool'."

I knew it was a taunt, but let it go. "What do you say, we go hunting for some more of these bones? Where did you say you picked it up from?"

"Outside the kitchen of Mount Everest Hotel."

It was a long hike to the famous hotel, but a worthwhile one. There were tonnes of bones and very few to share with. In any case, with Raja nearby, I didn't have to worry about bullies. You see I am very small in size, and Raja is the toughie of the town.

"If only it wasn't this far, I'd come here for all my meals," Raja confessed making the most of his infrequent visits.

Suddenly, the backdoor of the kitchen flew open and two men stepped out.

"As your manager I must warn you that if you do not concentrate on your work, you will be dismissed." The older man was well dressed and though he spoke these words sternly, he obviously cared for the younger man.

"I am sorry, sir, my mind just isn't in my work. Ever since I heard the news about Anjali's secret wedding, nothing matters to me any longer." The young man, a handsome young man at that, was a picture of despair.

"Well, you got to snap out of it Andy. Or it will lead to your downfall".

Anjali? Andy? Wedding? Sounded familiar. If this Andy's name was Andrew, it had to be the young couple Trixy was talking about.

"Lets get out of here," suggested Raja,. "before they chase us out."

"No, wait a moment. I want to hear more." I needed some icebreakers to get back into Trixy's good books.

The manager put a hand on Andy's shoulder affectionately. "Listen son, you are still young...very young. I am sure you'll find someone else you will be happier with and…"

"No!!" Andy retorted strongly. Suddenly, a steely look crept into his eyes. "If Anjali marries anyone else…*I'll commit suicide!"*

The bone fell out of my mouth.

Later, when I went to Trixy's house, I felt as though an Arctic glacier had suddenly moved in. The ice-cold shoulder I got from Trixy made the Darjeeling winter seem like a Kolkata summer. All my attempts to resume a normal conversation failed. Finally I played my trump card.

"Okay, if you don't want to hear about Andrew's reaction when he heard about Anjali's wedding, its fine by me." I started walking away.

She darted in like an arrow and stood two inches away from my nose. "Andrew knows?"

"That's what I say. But if you insist on behaving like a frozen…"

"What did he say? How did you know where he is? What's he going to do?" The questions came like bullets from an AK47.

"He is going to commit suicide."

The words devastated her. "WHAT? The poor dear!" she exclaimed, tears welling in her eyes. "We must do something! We have got to help them!"

"Help him? Why should we help him commit suicide?"

"Not help him commit suicide, *stupid*. Help them overcome this disastrous situation," she shouted angrily. She muttered to herself, mimicking me, "help him commit suicide..." And just as quickly jumped back at me. "See what happens hanging around with that dumb mongrel. You become dumb too!"

"Don't bring my friend into this," I warned, still unsure how Raja got blamed for a young relationship gone astray.

"So what do we do now?" Trixy got back on track. "I know, let's go to Queeny and tell her about the situation. She'll know what to do."

"Queeny? Never heard of her."

"If you have the time to get away from that brute, you will find there is a whole new world out there besides him." She really must detest poor Raja. And he has never even harmed her. "For your information, Queeny is Anjali's bulldog. A very beautiful and sweet-natured dog, and a very good friend of mine."

So off we went to meet this divine creature. My first impression of her was miles away from Trixy's description. In fact it was just the opposite. With her beady eyes, wrinkled face and drooling mouth she had to be the most ugly dog I had met till date. Beautiful?

She looked at me suspiciously. "Who is this?"

"Cocky," explained Trixy, a little embarrassedly. "Remember I told you about him?"

"Not at all suitable for you," she gave her judgement, looking at me as though I was something even cats wouldn't touch. "He looks so…so ordinary." With that she turned round and ignored me totally.

Not so sweet-natured either.

"I have bad news, Queeny," interrupted Trixy, glad to change the subject. In a few selected words the latest position was posted to Queeny.

"That's really bad," Queeny agreed. "And he is so handsome." What that was supposed to mean, I couldn't understand. "And that village boy Ravi, who she is being married off to, is a known goonda and a malicious person. The Apso friend I have from the same village told me he is a real wicked man and is only after Shekharbabu's money. How Shekharbabu can make such a mistake, is beyond me."

"Isn't there anything we can do about it?"

"Well, as I can't speak their language I can't warn them either, can I?" First sensible thing she said till now. "But if I can…"

A shrill scream filled the air and Anjali's mother came running out of the house. "SHE'S RUN AWAY!! Anjali has left a note saying if she can't marry Andy, she'll never return to this place!"

After the initial shock, Anjali's parents started regretting their stern stand against Andrew. "This is far, far worse than allowing her to marry Andrew," Shekharbabu lamented, holding his head in his hands. The police were immediately informed and a hunt was launched. They searched the road to Siliguri, enquiring at every small town and village, but nobody seemed to have seen her. By evening, after all efforts failed to catch up with her someone suggested, "if you really don't mind her marrying Andrew, why don't you put a small message in the newspaper clarifying your decision? If she reads it she'll come back home immediately."

It seemed like the only alternative so the family and friends set about wording the message. After a number of rough drafts a final one was selected and immediately despatched to the newspaper's office.

"No use," said Queeny despondently. "She hates reading newspapers. 'It's only full of bad news, "she used to say. And they're all looking in the wrong places for her. I think I know where to find her."

Trixy and I had stayed back to see if we could be of any help, though of course what kind of help, we had no idea.

"If you know where she may be, why don't we go there? We could persuade her to come back," said Trixy, brightly.

"Aren't you forgetting something, honey? We can't talk!"

"Wait a minute," said I, after keeping mum all evening. I had held back my wisdom till now, to avoid being criticised by the over-smart Queeny. "There are many drafts of the newspaper message still on the table. If we hand over one copy to Anjali, maybe she'll understand."

Queeny contemplated the idea and conceded. "Not bad…for a guy of his size. I think it is a good idea."

"So let's go," cried Trixy excitedly, jumping on the table and selecting a draft.

"Wait a minute...wait a minute," cautioned Queeny. "It's already dark outside, and where I feel Anjali is hiding, is far away and a lonely place. It may be dangerous going off on our own now. Considering we are two young ladies and only this...this...little fellow to protect us..."she left it to us to complete her thought.

Now I was really miffed. I wanted to remind her that size never mattered and that I can be ferocious too, as and when the situation demanded. And that, with her around no protection was really required, as surely no one in his right mind would choose to bother her. But all this explanation could mean a waste of time, and that was one commodity we were falling short of. So instead, I suggested, "why don't we call Raja? He could join us."

"Now who is Raja?"

"You don't want to know," Trixy informed wryly. "He is the local toughie, and regretfully, Cocky's best friend."

"Sounds interesting. Let's give it a try."

Have you heard of love at first sight? Queeny just demonstrated it to us later. On meeting Raja, her drooling took on new a tempo and cups of saliva drooled down every minute, her beady eyes rolled on as though she was on a roller coaster, and...she actually smiled.

Raja gallantly agreed to join us and we instantly set off down a winding trail, with Queeny in the lead.

"What's wrong with that Queeny? Why has she got that silly smile on her face all the time? And why is she continuously looking at me only, instead of the path ahead. It's making me nervous." Raja did look agitated as he heaped on the questions.

I let him figure it out for himself. But knowing him, and knowing his knowledge of love matters, I was sure he'd be able to figure it all out latest by the turn of the century.

"Where exactly are you taking us?" I asked as we left the town behind and kept moving deeper into the wilderness.

"There is a monastery about eight kilometres from the town. Its name is Ging Monastery and is said to be the oldest in Darjeeling. In fact Darjeeling even didn't exist when it was consecrated in 1818, as at that time this region was in Sikkim. The Head Lama at the monastery is also from Sikkim. It's quite secluded but Anjali loves it, and used to often bring me along with her." Then to the rest she added, "from now on it could get dangerous, so be alert."

It sure was a bit scary, scampering through such wild hillside, even though the moon helped us on our way. Besides the cold it was the eerie effects of long shadows cast by dark trees that sent an occasional shiver up my spine.

We kept a constant watch for wild animals. Occasionally a pack of wild dogs would come in view, but seeing Raja they'd stop in their tracks. And further seeing Queeny, they'd quickly hop back to wherever they came out from.

When we reached the monastery we were all out of breath, but seeing the structure serenely lit by the moon whose light aesthetically illuminated its beautiful architecture, we were glad we made the trip. It projected a spiritual and peaceful ambience, as all holy places are meant to, though very few actually do.

"Queeny!" Anjali exclaimed happily, when we found her in the main hall. "How did you know...oh I am so glad to see you." She picked Queeny up and actually hugged her and planted a dozen kisses on her, God bless her, before seeing the rest of us. "Your friends?"

Trixy, who was carrying the message stepped forward and placed it at Anjali's feet. Queeny had wanted the honour of carrying it, but we voted against it. With her continuous drooling the message would probably have been washed away.

Anjali squealed with happiness upon reading the message. Without wasting further time we made our trip back along with Anjali.

Immediately upon Anajli's return things returned to normal at her house. The marriage with Ravi was cancelled, obviously not without embarrassment from her parents' side, and a new date was fixed for Anjali and Andrew's wedding. All four of us were invited as guests of honour. But three days before the marriage, disaster struck. Andrew was arrested for theft. One of the guests in his hotel was robbed of his belongings.

"Impossible!" Queeny thundered, when we next met, her many layered wrinkles quivering in agreement. "I've known him for sometime now and I am sure he couldn't have done it."

"But the fact remains," I reminded, "the police found all the stolen goods in his room."

"That room in the hotel is a common room. He shares it with other stewards and uses it for just a few hours every day. It has to be the work of some other steward."

Then came the evidence that part of the loot was also found on Andrew's person. There was foreign currency in his wallet and a jewelled pendant in his pocket. And a box of expensive jewellery still remained untraced.

That put an end to all speculations about Andrew's innocence, and also an end to his marrying Anjali.

"Thank God this came to light before my daughter could marry him," said a relieved Shekharbabu. "Else the name of my family would have been rubbed in mud. Now she will have to marry Ravi."

As the day's events unwound one by one, Anjali's mood also changed accordingly. Upon first hearing of Andrew's arrest, she vociferously protested. When his involvement became certain, she became sullen. And when her marriage to Ravi was once again announced, she simply became speechless. Shocked and dumbstruck, she refused to come out of her room and we all feared for her safety.

We, the newly formed foursome were at our wits' end trying to figure out what we should do. The only good thing coming out of it all was a quiet acceptance of Raja by Trixy. Now that Queeny had taken a liking to Raja, it became a regular sight for the four of us to be seen together. Strangely, and I should say very strangely, we discovered that Raja had started taking a bath daily these last few days, and altogether he looked much better groomed. When I commented on the subject he suddenly became touchy and gruffly asked, "anything wrong in looking clean?"

That same evening, Ravi came calling. We were all there and just as there is love at first sight there must be hatred at first sound too. His high-pitched, over-caring falsetto voice brought our hair standing on its ends. We took an instant dislike to him as he walked into the house with a leering grin. I noticed a black terrier had followed him, and he was leering at Trixy. Like master, like dog!

I had a sudden idea.

"Why don't you pretend to befriend him?" I suggested to Trixy.

"Cocky!! *How dare you!*"

"Hear me out," I protested. "He may disclose something...something wicked about his master. If we have such facts, may be we can convince Shekharbabu to once again withdraw this marriage proposal."

Trixy looked at me angrily.

"We are all here to protect you if he gets overfriendly," I pushed.

After much pleading and convincing she did agree to give it a try. "But don't bank on a result," she warned. "I know his type. His tongue won't wag as readily as his tail."

But for once she was wrong. In five minutes she had him eating out of her hands...er, paws. "Oh, Ravi is a great master," the terrier boasted. "Just the kind I like. Won't take no for an answer. Just look at this Anjali case." Queeny's hair bristled at the mention of her mistress's name. "She said 'no' to Ravi and wanted to marry someone else. But Ravi won't tolerate such a rebuke, so he..." he stopped mid-sentence as though he had already spoken too much.

"So what did he do?" four pairs of ears strained to hear the faintest whisper from him.

"Naaa...can't tell you. It might land him in trouble." Tough luck I thought, slackening my ears.

"Your master has only enough brains to cover the tip of a pin," goaded Queeny, stepping towards him menacingly. "He couldn't do a thing to win over my mistress."

"Well he did get to her, didn't he?" he said with a mischievous grin.

"It was fate that she lost her true love." Queeny fought gallantly, now inches away from sinking her deadly teeth into him. "If it wasn't fate, she'd have..."

"Fate, my hind feet!" he sneered. "It was my master that saw to it that Andrew went to jail, which cleared his own way."

Stunned, we all fell silent. But I knew that it's always wise to strike while the iron is hot. "That's one big lie! How could he have sent Andrew to jail? Andrew is there because he was..."

"Framed!!" he said emphatically.

The words just hung there as we all exchanged glances.

"It was my master's idea to frame Andrew and get him out of the way," he continued.

"I don't believe you," I continued with my act. "How could your master, who was miles away from the scene of crime, steal those valuables from one hotel room and place it in another? And even put some of the stolen articles into Andrew's clothing."

"You guys are obviously morons! You don't know anything! He didn't have to do it. His friend Hari, who also works in the hotel, did everything. It was easy as taking candy from a child," he said.

Or, easy as making you talk, thought I. So that's what happened and that's how Andrew lost Anjali.

Having shared his knowledge the terrier renewed paying attention to Trixy. She backed away, Queeny stepped forward, I growled as deeply as I could and Raja just looked on challengingly. It was enough to discourage him and he moved on seeking his master.

"So that's it!!" cried Queeny excitedly after Ravi's dog left. "Poor Andrew is innocent, and this vile creature, Ravi, framed him to get to Anjali. How can anyone be so wicked…and they call us beasts."

"What's more important now is to decide what we should do with this piece of explosive information," said I, assuming leadership of the group. "First of all we are not sure if that terrier spoke the truth. He could very well have cooked up a story just to impress us. Let's put our four heads together and work out a course of action." I should have said 'three' heads, as Raja, though possessed of a head, never knew it, and as such never used it. His was a world of instincts and brute strength.

"Let Raja decide. He is the head of our group."

That came out of the blue. I looked at Queeny to see if she was joking.

"Don't be silly. Raja cannot decide beyond when to sleep and when to eat," said Trixy coming over and standing next to me, to show whose side she was on.

"If that's what you think," replied Queeny glaring at Trixy, "then you go on listening to this...this...little fellow and I'll be with him." She walked over to Raja's side. The battle lines drawn, the issue of Andrew and Anjali took a backseat.

Poor Raja looked at as though we were discussing Homer's Iliad. Totally lost. He looked towards me imploringly. I was about to go to him when Trixy's cold cough warned me off. They say, Phantom's voice can freeze the blood of a lion, but Trixy's voice I am sure, could freeze Phantom himself.

"Cocky, let's go for a walk to the mall," she said softly, which was always more dangerous.

"Good idea," said Raja happily, and trotted towards us.

"RAJA!!" this was no cold response from Queeny. It was a harsh, direct command a Sergeant Major of the Marines Corps would have been proud of. Raja responded like a cadet. Quickly returning back behind the invisible dividing line.

As we separated and walked on our own way, I wondered if the argument was really about whether Raja or I should be the leader of this pack. Or…

"What now?" I asked of Trixy as we moved about aimlessly around The Mall. "We know Andrew is innocent, but how do we help him in getting released?"

"I never knew she could be so bossy," replied Trixy crossly, totally on another plane of thought. "And to think I considered her my best friend."

"To come back to the problem at hand," I reminded her, "how do we help Andrew?" I thought that was pretty selfish of her to indulge in her own hang-ups when there was a major problem at hand.

"Ravi's friend, Hari the steward, seems to be our only answer. If we can get him to confess, Andrew will be released." Not that selfish after all.

"But how?"

"Lets go to Mount Everest hotel. May be we'll find some clue there."

All the way to the hotel, Trixy continued with her anti-Queeny campaign. "Can you believe it?" To stop her from continuing, I agreed to believe her. "It was thanks to me that she met Raja!" Oh, really? "And she treats me this way?" Actually she treated herself that way. "Really, Raja deserved someone better!" That took the cake.

It was dinnertime when we reached the hotel. The beauty of its majestic, palace-like architecture was further

accentuated by special lighting arrangements, which gave it a fairy-tale like look. We hung around the kitchen door and overheard the staff gossiping over the day's events.

"Never thought he'd do anything like that."

"But why would Andrew want to steal? He was not rich, but he was not short of money either."

"Remember, he was about to get married. One needs truckloads of money at such times."

"Poor guy…and he had it in him to go all the way to the top."

Besides some delicious leftovers, we didn't pick up any useful tip or clues. "Wonder which one is Hari." There were scores of uniformed staff busily hurrying about their jobs. Apparently there is nothing more urgent than serving hungry human beings. Amidst a multitude of voices, ranging from gossip, to requests and commands, Trixy picked "Hari, table No. 7 wants the bill."

We sneaked into one of the side rooms and identified table No. 7, and then, Hari. He seemed to be from the plains and looked efficient, smart and well-mannered.

Later, upon completing his duties he checked his watch. It was past 11 pm. Time to retire for the day. He removed his jacket and tie and stepped out of the building. We were right behind him. He stretched and yawned and casually looked towards a cluster of pine trees, a hundred yards away. A cigarette lighter flickered in the distant darkness and he promptly walked towards it. A secret meeting? A man came out from behind the trees as Hari neared him. It was Ravi.

No further evidence was needed about Andrew's innocence. We quickly got into position for their secret meeting. It was getting to be very cold, so Trixy and I got as close as we could to each other for warmth. Normally this kind of environment...moonlit open grounds, peaceful surroundings and the sweet smell of pine trees would have taken us both on a romantic trip. But today we were tensed-up and concentrated totally on the task at hand.

"Well done Hari. Your reward." We heard Ravi as he passed on a small packet to Hari.

"Thanks. I would have done the job without this reward anyway. Now that Andrew is out of the way, I will be automatically promoted to the rank of Senior Steward."

"Scoundrels!!" growled Trixy, unable to control herself.

"Who is that??" Ravi charged towards us, his lighter flickering. He spotted us and relaxed. He kicked into thin air and shooed us away.

We walked by the kitchen door and waited for Hari to return. When he did, we followed him confidently, as though we were the owners of the hotel. He opened the door to room No. 209 on the second floor. It was dark inside. I knew this was our chance, so without warning Trixy, I streaked into the room and dived under the bed. He shut the door and switched on the light. I was safe inside and Trixy was left behind in the corridor wondering what happened to me.

Suddenly, a yell was heard from outside the door, *"a wild dog!!"* Soon poor Trixy was chased by every steward, bearer and manager of the hotel. At least, I consoled myself; it would take her mind off Queeny.

In the room, Hari took off his shoes and stretched himself. Framing must be an exhausting job, I thought. He shuffled to the large mirror and studied himself intently. He brushed aside some hair from his forehead, adjusted his eyebrows and tweaked his nose. Taking a step back he grinned, pleased with what he saw.

Suddenly, Hari dropped to his knees and peered under the bed. I panicked. The game was up and there was no place for me to run. I got ready to demonstrate my most ferocious growl, (Trixy had a good laugh when I had tried to scare her once).

Hari blindly groped under the bed for something and pulled out a box. Unbelievingly, he didn't even see me. He carried the box to the table and opened it. I couldn't see what it contained, but it must have been good as his eyes dazzled with excitement. He reached in and picked out something long. It was a huge glittering necklace. His other hand was lovingly rubbing a large ruby ring.

This must be the missing jewel box! If only the police could see this. But first I must get out of here. The door was closed and the windows were shut too. There was no way out.

Hari, satisfied with his trophy, pushed the case back under the bed, switched off the lights and got into bed. A little later, I ventured out from under the bed. The room was locked as I guessed, so I checked out the bathroom. There was a ventilator in there but it was too high for me. I did try to reach it, but unsuccessfully. I saw no other connecting rooms and found myself trapped! Would I now have to wait for morning? I returned to the room and hunted for ideas. Pretty soon I hit upon one.

There was a shoe brush lying under the table. I picked it up in my mouth, went to the front door and tapped it twice.

"Who is that?" jumped up Hari, as I took refuge under a settee close to the door. He walked up to the door barefooted and cautiously opened it. No one. He stepped outside to check properly and I took my chance. While his head was turned towards one side, I bolted for the other. Two minutes and three close shaves later, I was out from the kitchen door and into the open grounds again. I looked around for Trixy and found her licking her foot painfully.

"If I ever get a chance, that fat bearer is going to regret he kicked me so hard." Good, I thought. Queeny needed the break.

I quickly updated her with the latest news. "Great! Now we can catch him red-handed," she said forgetting her pain. "But...but...as Queeny used to say, 'aren't we forgetting something?'" I couldn't believe it. She was already missing her friend.

"Yes, we can't talk, but I know someone who understands me. First thing in the morning, I'll make her help us."

On our way back we bumped into Raja and Queeny. "Where have you two been? We looked everywhere for you."

Trixy was about to do her cold-shoulder act, when Queeny's next words hit us like a sledgehammer. "Anjali has tried to commit suicide! She took some poison. The doctor has cleaned her stomach and given her some medicine but it is not working. He says till she cooperates the medicine won't work. If her condition persists, he says, she could be dead by morning."

We took in this shocking news terribly.

Trixy looked at me imploringly. "Andrew must be released from the prison immediately. We can't wait till morning. If we can bring him back to her soon, she will automatically revive."

We told a puzzled Queeny and Raja to return to Anjali, as we were handling the Andrew side.

Divya, my young mistress, mumbled something, pulled her blanket up again, turned round and went back to sleep. I once again caught the blanket in my mouth (you should try it someday to understand how awful it is), and pulled it down. This was taking longer than I expected. If Andrew didn't meet Anjali by morning, and show all is well with him and that they could get married, she would die. And Divya was the only one who could help us rescue Andrew.

"What's wrong with you?" Divya snapped viciously, covering herself with the blanket for the third time. "Do it one more time, and I'll get up and wallop you," she warned. Divya, as already mentioned is my mistress, and my favourite human being. She is the elder child of the Pradhans, the other being Vishnu. If there was one person who could understand me, it had to be Divya. Though right now, it didn't seem so.

I started barking. Divya promptly threw her slipper at me and pulled her pillow tightly over her head. Trixy, who was standing close by, commented wryly, "If you call that 'understanding you', I'd hate to be around when she misunderstands you." Some more urgent barking and a shout came from above, her parent's room. "He probably needs to go out!" her father called out.

With sleepy eyes Divya checked the alarm clock by her bedside. "It's two in the morning, you little nut-case. Where were you all day?" She lazily got up, pulled a woollen gown over her night suit, grumbling and muttering all the time. Then she noticed my urgent action of asking her to follow me. "WHAT?? You want me to play games with you? *Now?*" she asked incredulously. "I'll kill you right now if that's the case!" And she sounded as though she meant it too.

But soon she did realise what I wanted. "Follow you? Is Vishnu in trouble again?" she asked worriedly. And then noticing Trixy she asked hesitatingly, "what are you two up to? Okay, okay, you want me to go out with you? Okay, I'll come...but it had better be good."

She opened the front door and as quickly shut it. "Brrrrr...that's very, very cold. I hope this is all worth it, Cocky...or you've had it."

She put on some more layers of clothing, picked up a torch and followed us out. As we trotted down the deserted street, Queeny came up near me and said, "I hope you know what you are doing, because I don't."

Doubting Thomas's everywhere! Where has something called 'faith' gone? "If you can think of something better," I offered, "I'll be happy to call this off." That kept her quiet.

"Slow down, slow down you two, I've got just two legs, remember? Ah...thank God you have stopped." Divya stood along side us, panting. "Where are we...Oh, right in front of Ramesh uncle's house." Ramesh uncle was a Police Inspector at the local police station.

"Clear your vocal chords and bark as loudly as you can," I advised Trixy, and started the ball rolling.

"What? Are you mad? You want us shot down? Didn't you hear Divya say this is Ramesh uncle's house?" As Trixie protested, poor Divya looked on, shell-shocked.

But it was too late to control me, and soon Trixy grudgingly joined in. Windows opened from neighbouring houses, abuses and curses were showered on us and even the occasional brickbat was tossed at us. Suddenly, at the inspector's house a window was thrown open and a powerful voice called out.

"WHO IS THAT AND WHAT'S GOING ON DOWN THERE?"

"Now you've done it, you barking ass! That's Ramesh uncle, and he'll now demonstrate to us the meaning of getting mad."

Sure enough a minute later the inspector charged out of his house, his baton ready to strike.

"Its me, Divya, and I am trying to keep this..."

Enough of wasting time! I had in front of me the man I wanted. I went up to him and pulled at his pyjamas. Then I enacted the full sequence of 'follow-me' drill.

"What...what does he want?" the inspector demanded.

"I think he wants you to follow him. He brought me here the same way and I think he has something to show us."

The inspector thought it over for a minute. "He has been useful to us earlier, if I remember correctly. So okay, let's see what he wants to show us."

With that he went back indoors and returned in five minutes, fully dressed and armed.

"Okay, lead the way doggy. We'll follow in a jeep."

And so I took them to Mount Everest hotel and to room No. 209 and to the jewel box. It was immediately identified by the manager as the stolen one. Hari was arrested.

"*HOW DID YOU STEAL THIS? WHO ELSE IS IN THIS RACKET?*" the inspector yelled, roughing up Hari.

Hari instantly paled and trembled with fear for his pretty face. "Don't hit me! Please don't hit me, I'll confess to everything."

And he did! Much to everyone's surprise he even cleared Andrew's name and implicated Ravi.

They immediately took him to the police station and released Andrew as well. Trixy and I once again forced Divya and Andrew to follow us. This time it did not require any enacting of my routine. We led them to Anjali's house and finally the two lovers met, one just recovered from oblivion, and the other about to enter it.

In her subconscious state Anjali realised Andrew was with her and that he was released from jail, and that they could soon get married.

At the stroke of dawn, she opened her eyes and smiled.

"Wow!! What excitement! What romance!" exclaimed Queeny happily, when we all met later that day. After Anjali had revived and was reunited with her loved one, and after we had dried our eyes, we indulged in two of our favourite pass times...eating and sleeping; something we had forgotten about, for almost twenty-four hours. "What an adventure that was. I'll never forget it."

"What I still don't understand..." began Raja with a far out look. In fact he hadn't understood a single thing that had taken place this last one day.

"Its okay dear," Queeny cut him off. "I'll explain it all to you...some day. So she turned to us, just shows what good team work can achieve."

I was about to protest but Trixy spoke first.

"Exactly," said Trixy, surprising me. Warming up to her friend once again, she continued. "When is the wedding..."

As the two friends chatted, Raja looked at me morosely. I knew he no longer enjoyed being 'domesticated', so I winked and asked him, "Want to go out on our own?"

He didn't need to answer as the two of us once again hit the road together. We heard the two surprised girls call out to us. But we pretended not to hear and happily returned to our old ways.

❑❑❑

5

To Save a Poltergeist

"MUMMY!! I can't find my walkman," called out Karishma's friend, Priyanka.

Karishma was spending the Sunday afternoon with her friend, studying the nuances of climatic changes in the subcontinent. Having completed, or rather given up trying to understand the subject, they were looking for some entertainment.

Mrs Chopra, Priyanka's mother, walked into the room, seemingly irritated at her daughter's carelessness. She was dressed to go out, as she was wearing a glittering silk saree and equally glittering jewellery. "I saw it on your table this morning."

"Well it isn't there now."

"Er...may be Little Pinku has put it somewhere else..."

"Who?"

"Er...sorry...nothing..."

"Mummy, who in God's name is 'Little Pinku'?"

"I told you, nobody." She saw the puzzled look from both girls and tried explaining. "I was thinking of something else. So you two..."

"Mummy, who were you talking about? You've never mentioned any such name before."

The stern look on Priyanka's face made her mother wilt and confess guiltily, "He's the mischievous ghost of the house...a sort of a poltergeist...that too not an absolute poltergeist. They say poltergeists normally are noisy spirits that throws things about. Little Pinku, as you know, is neither noisy nor does he throw things around. He simply likes to hide things."

Both the girls sat bolt upright, mouths wide open. "Po...po...po...po..."

"Oh, nothing to be so scared about. He has never harmed anyone. Here, help me with this necklace."

"Wh...what are you talking about, mummy? Ghosts, in this house? I've never..."

"We've kept it from you. You see when we bought this place three years ago, we apparently inherited the house ghost too."

"WHAT?" Priyanka and Karishma jumped off the bed they were relaxing on and stood very close to Mrs Chopra.

"Tch!! I told you he is harmless. That little boy was apparently one of the occupants of this flat many years ago. Even the previous occupants knew of him. We do not know how he died, but he obviously did not want to leave this house. All he does is shift and hide little things in the house."

Maya, their maid for three years and who had now come into the room and over heard the conversation put in her bit too. "Madam is right. Things in the kitchen keep shifting from one place to another regularly," she confirmed fear showing in her eyes. She was middle-aged, kind-faced and quiet, and displayed motherly love to Priyanka.

Priyanka's eyes were bulging almost to the point of popping out. "But...but..."

"Yes, we always cover for him as it may have scared you. Then again, we've never been sure if he really could be the culprit as we misplace things ourselves very often. And of course, no one has seen him till date. But now you are big enough..."

" 'I *may* have got scared?' Mummy I am *terrified.* I...I..."

"It's okay, Priyanka," stepped in Karishma, much to Mrs Chopra's relief. "If he hasn't done anything to frighten you in three years, then may be your mum is right. There is nothing to fear."

"Are you kidding? Then you come and stay here; I'll move over to your place. And...and...I am going to be alone tonight?" Her father and mother were going to go out to a wedding party.

It took another hour for Mrs Chopra and Karishma to somewhat convince Priyanaka that she was over-reacting. But it still didn't ease her mind. She was visibly shaken and seemed jumpy, and automatically got hooked on to the habit of first checking every part of the room before entering it. She also learnt to jump three feet high at the drop of a pin.

"So, have you met him yet?" Karishma gleefully asked Priyanka next morning, at school. The cold disgusted look she got in response conveyed that her sense of humour was not particularly appreciated.

"The good part is that mummy cannot find her diamond necklace that she wore last night. Serves her right for being so smug with us yesterday."

"That diamond necklace? That must have been expensive?"

"Yes, her wedding jewellery. Yesterday mummy had gone to the bank and removed the necklace from her bank locker. She was to have replaced it this morning, but till she could go to the bank she had kept it in her bedside table drawer, as she always did. But surprisingly, after her bath when she opened the drawer…the necklace was not there. Unfortunately, she doesn't seem to be too concerned as she knows she'll find it sooner or later in some other place."

"Gulp! That's scary, if not downright weird. First your walkman, and now an expensive necklace. This poltergeist seems to have expensive tastes…or is it at all the poltergeist? What about your maid, Maya? Is she trustworthy?"

"Of course!" Priyanka sounded confident. "In three years we have had no reason to suspect her of being a thief."

Next day, Karishma faced a more worried-looking Priyanka.

"The necklace is still not found. We've looked simply everywhere."

"May be you should inform the police."

"That's what daddy says too, but mummy firmly believes it will turn up on its own."

"And...any sign of...er...your...Little Pinku?" Try as she may, Karishma could not suppress the creeping smile as she said the name.

"Not funny! And no, thankfully no sign of him either."

"Then may be, its time I entered the scene," said Karishma dramatically, eyes gleaming with excitement at the thought of solving another mystery. It had been some time since her last 'case', and the extended lean period was beginning to tell on her. She was thirsting for a new adventure. "Today after school I'll accompany you home, and make a proper investigation of the crime scene."

Later that day, after investigating all the rooms in Priyanka's house, Karishma sat by the window, deep in thought.

"And your verdict, Madam Detective?" asked Mrs Chopra, quite amused at the young girl's seriousness.

"Either the necklace is still in the house, or it is an inside job."

"Inside job? You mean one of us is the suspect?" the bemused smile still lingered on Mrs Chopra's face.

"One of you, or someone else you trust and who has access to your rooms."

"The only other person in our house, besides the three of us, is Maya. And we trust her totally."

"But she becomes my prime suspect." Karishma was convinced that this case had a short life as she zeroed in on Maya. A pity because she was itching for something more challenging...more juicy!

"But Madam Detective, Maya comes to work at ten in the morning. The necklace was found missing by me at 8 a.m." Mrs Chopra seemed to be enjoying proving Karishma wrong.

"Oh! Well...in that case...I think...er...I'll need some time." A flustered Karishma quickly disappeared into another room, promising herself never to be so conclusive in future.

As Priyanka joined Karishma, she sat down at a table and tried reorganising her facts.

"From the facts at hand it is certain that this case has to lead us to either of two totally different ends...Little Pinku, or someone who knows that something valuable was easily accessible in your house for a short period of time. That...er...again narrows down the field to just...er. Tell me Priyanka, is your father's financial position...okay?"

"WHAT? How dare you suspect my father? I think you'd better, this instant, leave my..."

"Sorry, sorry, sorry! I am really sorry Priyanka. That was stupid of me. It is just that the situation looks so impossible. Whew, this case is going to drive me nuts…and I thought it was an open and shut one."

Karishma, now red in face, cursed herself for being so tactless and thoughtless. "Okay, so let's return to the original logic." Priyanka now realised why her friend was popularly known as 'Crazy Krish'. Too impulsive and too aggressive!

"It could be Little Pinku, continued Karishma, or someone…else."

"I think you've already mentioned that about two hundred times."

"So let's start with Little Pinku. What do we know about him?"

"Exactly nothing. And all mum knows is what she has told us already…next to nothing."

"Okay, you find out the address of the previous occupants, and let's do some visiting

The Kukude family, the previous occupants of Priyanka's flat, now lived in the outskirts of Pune, at Vimannagar. A comparatively new settlement, it was a peaceful and quiet place.

"Little Pinku?" asked Mrs Kukude, after introductions were completed. "Why do you want to know about the poor boy? He had such a tragic end to his life. It would be better to let him rest in peace." An overtly plump lady, Mrs Kukude seemed to have a soft corner for the boy.

"But he is not letting us rest in peace," reminded an agitated Priyanka. "Why is he still haunting that house?"

"That's a long story," she answered with a sad look on her face. "Please come in and I'll tell you all about him."

Mrs Kukude offered them some light refreshments, helping herself to some first. "He does not exactly haunt, you know," she said, giving Priyanka a disapproving glance. "But to answer your question we'll have to go back a few years. About fifteen years ago, Pinku and his family lived in that house, built by his father. It was a happy family with Pinku the normal mischievous boy. I believe his favourite game was pinching little articles from the house and hiding them elsewhere. It used to drive his mother mad they say, but he apparently enjoyed making them search the house. Ha, ha, ha...what a dear boy he must have been." She paused for a moment but that was enough to half empty the plate of '*chiwda*'. The girls were yet to taste it.

She continued, "Then, when he was about twelve, he went to the seaside at Alibagh for a school holiday, along with other boys. Some boys say they saw him step into the sea, waste high...too high for a non-swimmer. Some boys remember him walking towards the rocks close to the sea. In any case, in the evening when the roll call was under way, Pinku was missing. They searched the beach and they looked for him in the rocky areas too. But no sign of him! Naturally the police were called in and a thorough search was made, but to no avail. Next morning, when his frantic parents came to the sea resort, one of the boys gave a fresh piece of information."

In one quick movement Mrs Kukude picked up the plate, emptied the *'chiwda'* into her podgy left hand, which in a flash slapped into her open mouth. The girls looked on apprehensively, but didn't mind as the story had caught their full attention.

"And this fresh piece of news was...?" Prompted Karishma.

"The boy said that he had earlier noticed a couple of thugs near the rocks, and they seemed to be suspiciously checking on the boys. And so the theory of kidnapping took shape. The distraught parents returned home expecting a ransom call, refusing to believe that the boy could have drowned. Their suspicion soon changed to certainty, as no body was recovered. They were convinced he was kidnapped and the ransom demand would soon come by. Days passed and then weeks, but there was no sign of either a ransom note, or Little Pinku. The police confirmed that they caught two shady looking thugs a few days later, but there was absolutely no suggestion of a kidnapping having been attempted. There was only one conclusion, but Pinku's parents preferred to live in hope.

"A few months passed yet his parents refused to accept the reality. 'He will return someday,' was their stubborn attitude. Er...you like some more *'chiwda'*? It's from Laxminarayan, you know. The best."

"No thanks." Karishma wanted to add 'just looking at it was quite enough'. But she was impatient to hear what happened next. "So what did the parents..."

"No, I must get you something to eat first." Mrs Kukude happily wobbled back to the kitchen and soon returned with a plateful of Shrewsbury biscuits and some *'bhakerwadi'*, a popular Maharashtrian savoury.

"So," she said, picking up three of the biscuits together "their relatives and friends got worried as the little boy's last rites were still not performed. They reminded the parents about it and then insisted that some prayers ought to be performed as is normally done for the dead. Try these biscuits, they are delicious." Having finished her share she offered them the plate. "They're from Kayani...the best."

"Er...not now...may be later, thanks." The dark and sad story had obviously made the girls lose their appetite.

"Please don't be shy," she said as she picked up the remaining three biscuits. "So the parents were pressurised from all sides to conduct some prayers for peace of the departed soul, which they flatly refused. They hung on to their hope. A year later, they left Pune for good. They rented out the house to us and gave us a forwarding address, to be given to their beloved son when he returned."

The girls were almost in tears. "And...?"

"Well you know the rest. He did return, but not in his body. His restless soul returned home, and he still goes on doing what he liked most...play tricks on people. Please have some *'bhakerwadis'*. I get them from a special place here, and they are..."

"We know...the best. But no thank you". Karishma was disgusted with the woman's gluttony. "We must be leaving now." Both the girls got up and walked to the door. "And thank you for all the refreshments."

"Not at all. Not at all," said a contented Mrs Kukude, placing three of the *'bhakerwadis'* simultaneously in her vast mouth.

Later that night, Karishma couldn't get any sleep. She kept thinking of the tormented soul of a young boy she had never met. She didn't know much about religion and Hindu customs relating to death, but prayed that there was some way his soul could find peace.

Coming back to the problem at hand, the first part of her investigation had proved futile. The possibility of a poltergeist at work was still present. But if so, where could he have hidden the necklace?

The second part of her investigation was even more complex. Who could have possibly entered the bedroom, not bothered to either steal or disturb any other item, gone directly to the side table, opened the drawer and takes away only the necklace? It had to be somebody who knew of the necklace. She had to discount the family of three. She had already learnt the hard way that that possibility couldn't exist.

Maya, the maid! Every finger pointed at her, but her alibi was too strong. If she wasn't there, she couldn't possibly have stolen it.

At school a happy Priyanka greeted her. "Guess what? I found my walkman in a suitcase on top of my cupboard."

"What?" Karishma was stunned by the news. She was just about getting to accept that the missing items could not be the work of Little Pinku. "How did it get there?"

"Little Pinku, of course. So you can now stop worrying about thieves and police and…"

"May be, but what about the necklace?"

"Oh it will surface someday soon. We're sure of it now."

"Nope! I am still not convinced. Maybe my investigation pattern is wrong, maybe my ring of suspects is small, maybe I should consider other people too. Your laundry man?" she asked suddenly. "How often does he come into the house?"

"We don't have a laundry man. Mum washes the clothes in the washing machine." Priyanka looked suspiciously at her friend…she seemed unnecessarily flustered.

"And for ironing? Or do you do that in the house too?" asked Karishma, almost accusingly.

"The ironing man comes daily, but he never enters the house. We hand over and collect the clothes at the door itself."

"May be when you were not looking…"

"But he comes just before lunch. Hours after the necklace was found missing. Come on Karishma, get a grip on yourself. The world is not as full of convicts as you make it out to be."

Karishma felt deflated. She knew Priyanka was right and she was getting carried away. But the thought of Little

Pinku being blamed for a possible crime committed by someone else, did not gel with her well. This had to do with a physical, human theft, and she won't give up on that theory. But, she realised, she had to change her line of investigation.

After school, Karishma once again accompanied Priyanka back to her house. She asked Maya some casual questions, but found the answers equally casual and innocent. Soon Karishma herself was convinced she was barking up the wrong tree. She had to look elsewhere for an answer.

After tea, Maya left for the day and the two girls spent time listening to music. Though Karishma was more of an outdoor person she found herself attracted to a certain segment of Indian music...gazals. And since Priyanka had a decent collection of this kind of music, they often spent hours together.

Later, on her way back home in a bus, Karishma rued the lack of evidence in this case. Should she pursue it or let it take its course? She always felt more alive when she was on a hunt. All her faculties seemed to shift to top gear and there was certain briskness in her gait whenever an investigation was on. But now...

The bus halted at a stop and there among the newly boarding passengers was Maya. Her house was in this vicinity, Karishma knew. But where was she going now? Maybe another house for work, maybe to a friend or a relative's place, or may be... Karishma on an impulse decided to find out. Maya had not noticed her and Karishma slid lower in her seat.

Karishma's stop came soon, but she didn't alight. It was a matter of just some extra bus fare, but she will have clarified the one doubt still remaining in her suspicious mind.

The bus went far into the city and finally Maya got up. Karishma stayed back till Maya alighted, and then she herself jumped off from the moving bus. Maya still did not see her, and the hunt was on.

Maya entered a narrow alley and then a small passage. Karishma waited in the alley as she saw her prey enter a house. Suddenly, a commotion flared up in the house and a minute later Maya stormed out, pulling a dishevelled man by his sleeves. She was yelling at the top of her voice and after every few steps took a swipe at the man's head. Still in a fury, Maya and the protesting man disappeared down the street.

Karishma, who had now taken refuge behind a tree, stepped out, amazed at the ferocity of the generally mild-mannered Maya. She saw a shopkeeper chuckling to himself.

"Why was she so upset?" she asked him casually.

"She aught to be! She works her heart out all day, while her husband, gambles and drinks. This scene has been repeated many times over these last few months."

"You mean he doesn't work at all?"

"Of course not! Who would employ a no-good lout? He begs and borrows from one and all, including me, till he gets neck-deep in debts. But I must say, he has cleared all his dues earlier this week. Must have won a jackpot, or something."

...or something!!

Karishma walked fast, her heart beating faster, but her mind simply racing away with all the concoctions it could imagine.

But how was it done? Karishma reached home but her mind was still glued on Maya and her husband. If Maya had taken the necklace, how did she get her hands on it, considering that she had not been near the necklace before it disappeared? Though Karishma had the intuition that she was on the right track, it just didn't make any sense. So far everything lost in the house was found again. Even the walkman, which Karishma was convinced was stolen, had been in the house all along.

Next morning, firmly believing that her original diagnosis was more probable, Karishma left for school. Waiting for her at the gate was a worried looking Priyanka.

"This morning mummy's purse was missing. We searched everywhere but..."

"Maya! Where was she?"

"I told you she comes after ten. I left for school before that."

This was getting too complex for Karishma's liking. "And last evening, did your mother have the purse with her?"

"She is not sure. It's the purse she uses for petty expenses and daily bazaar. She couldn't find it in the morning when she wanted to pay the *'sabziwali'*."

Once again, Karishma accompanied Priyanka back to her house. What met their eyes there almost stunned them. Sitting at the dining table, drinking hot tea and having a hearty laugh were Mrs Chopra and Maya.

"You two seem to be celebrating something. You have found the necklace?" asked Priyanka hopefully.

"No, but we have found the purse. Little Pinku was at work again, ha, ha, ha." Mrs Chopra actually sounded happy discovering the poltergeist up to his pranks. "A little while ago, Maya found the purse in the kitchen cabinet. Can you imagine the tricks the little darling is up to? Come join us for some tea."

"Was there any money in it?" Karishma came straight to the point.

"Yes there was a hundred rupee note, a few ten rupee notes and some coins. It's all in there. Nothing missing" replied Mrs. Chopra.

"I tell you this little fellow has hidden your necklace some place too," put in Maya, with an equally benevolent expression on her face. "So don't bother about the police, the necklace will show up sooner or later, and from the least likely place."

"I think you're right, Maya. So Karishma dear, forget about your investigations too. There is nothing to worry about."

"If you say so…" muttered Karishma, dejectedly yet unconvincingly.

"So what should I be doing now…continue with the investigation, or…?" Karishma wondered as she left for home. Her instincts told her that Maya was not as innocent as she made herself look. But at the same time there is no overlooking the fact that nothing actually was missing from the house, except the necklace. And since Little Pinku was obviously behind all the temporary missing objects, then logically the missing necklace must be his handiwork too.

But just to stimulate her thinking she decided to go through the possibilities, assuming that Maya did take the necklace. As logic was not working she decided to switch over to a hypothetical case.

"So, if a poor person steals," she began analysing a possible scenario, "an expensive piece of jewellery what would he or she do with it? Selling it immediately would arouse suspicion, especially if the police were already looking for the thief. It would be a matter of time before he or she is caught. So, to make matters more interesting, as in the current scenario, what would happen if the police were not in the picture yet? Here to be on the safe side, the thug would probably hold on to his loot for some time at least, make sure the heat was off, before considering selling it."

But, what if he needed money urgently? Then he would of course risk selling it, or use the jewellery as a guarantee against a loan. Cash in hand, and jewellery too within his reach is exactly what he would have preferred. And if that's so, how should she unveil the truth? The answer, Karishma decided, was in forcing the issue.

"Krishna," she asked of her elder brother on returning home, "Have you ever considered acting?"

Krishna, who was valiantly tackling a difficult theorem, jerked his head up. "*What?*" He spat the word out in such a sharp tone as to make a simple 'what?' an incredulous *'what!'*

"Well, considering you are so...ahem...good looking, and...and..."

"HA!!" the exclamation couldn't have sounded crueller. "You must be thinking I am some kind of a fool, don't you? I mean obvious you are going to ask me for a favour, and you are just trying to flatter me with some stupid praises."

"Don't be silly. Would I do such a thing to my own brother? It's just that Priyanka's uncle, that famous film producer Yash Chopra, is visiting her and..."

"Yash Chopra is Priyanka's uncle?" Krishna jumped up in disbelief. Karishma was quite aware of her brother's keen interest in Bollywood affairs, as he spent most of his pocket money on film magazines.

"Didn't you know that? Well he is here and is looking for a boy for a small role in his latest film. But of course you won't be interested in such nonsense." She started walking off.

"Wait a minute, wait a minute." Krishna pulled her back by her arm. "I didn't know Yash Chopra was Priyanka's uncle. So about this small role, what do I ..."

Trapped!!

"But where is Mr Chopra?" Krishna, quite uncomfortable in the torn and dirty clothes he was made to wear, looked about him unhappily.

"I told you he would be watching your performance undetected. He does not want you to put up an act, which you will if you see him. This is just to help you act naturally." Karishma had managed to bring her brother to the slum area, where Maya lived knowing she would be at work at that time of the day. But the main task still lay ahead.

"I feel stupid standing here and approaching these people with your silly script."

"Just do it…if you want that role." Karishma had taken position close by, near the common water tap, and prayed her key suspect would show up fast…before her brother lost his patience.

"Excuse me, Sir," said Krishna, hurrying towards a common labourer. "Would you like to dispose off hot jewellery? Best price and no questions asked." He said it all in one breath, looking pleadingly at the man as though he was asking for candy.

"What?" snapped the man angrily.

Krishna gulped hard. "…er…would you like to…er…"

"Would you like a blow and a quick trip to the police station?" the man asked threateningly.

Krishna quickly retreated back to Karishma. "There, I did it. Now will you take me to Mr Yash Chopra?"

"Are you kidding? With that kind of performance he will not touch you with a ten-foot pole. Where was the mean look I told you to put on? Where was the toughness in your voice? And what was all that about 'Sir'? Did he look like a 'Sir'?"

"Okay, okay, so I can't do it. That was my third try and I failed again. So lets go back home."

Just then Karishma caught sight of Maya's husband. Her pulse began to race. "No! I'll give you one more chance to be the next Shahrukh Khan. So give your best shot. See that man there? Try convincing him and give him the slip of paper I gave you. He is Mr Chopra's own man."

Tired of this act Krishna grudgingly walked towards Maya's husband. This last time and then I'm going home, he decided.

"Hey!" he called out, trying to look as mean as he could. "Want to get rid of stolen jewellery? I know the place. Best prices and no questions asked."

First the man ignored him, but the moment he heard 'stolen jewellery', he stopped in his tracks.

"*What?* Who are you?" he demanded.

"Nobody you know," Krishna replied confidently. "But if you are interested, this is the address, and only between four and five in the evening." Krishna slipped the paper into the man's hand. It had an address scribbled on it. "And ask for Kalu," he whispered, dramatically.

"What does he want?" Another young man entered the scene. "I've been watching him and that girl there for sometime now, and I've never seen them here before."

"He is talking of some stolen jewellery." Maya's husband informed him.

"Is that so? He must be a thief!"

"No, no, no,...you are making a mistake," explained Krishna hastily. "This is just a film shooting and Yash Chopra is there..."

"Shooting?" said the young man with a sneer. "I do the shooting around here, particularly at boys with weird stories."

Karishma had seen and heard enough and knew they'd be in trouble any second now. *"Run Krishna, run!!"* she warned aloud.

"Why?" asked a calm Krishna. "Just tell them about Mr Chopra and..."

"You and your Mr Chopra...I'll..." the young man whipped out a knife and walked menacingly towards Krishna.

'RUN KRISHNA!! JUST RUN!!" panicked Karishma, herself running to help her brother, but Krishna needed no further prompting. The sight of the knife was enough to power his legs with speed Olympians can only dream of. In seconds the siblings were running for their lives as half the slum dwellers joined in the chase.

It was a good fifteen minutes of sprint before they felt safe. Leaning against a wall the two panted, trying to catch their breath.

"Why didn't you...tell them...about Mr Chopra?" asked the gullible Krishna between gasps.

"He...wasn't there." Karishma confessed, genuinely hating to lie to her brother. But the plan had worked. The address was now in Maya's husband's hands.

"What?"

"Must have been delayed. Anyway, the job was done. So thank you brother."

"What job?"

"Mrs Chopra said today that it was time to bring in the police," Maya nervously informed her husband. "She said Mr Chopra insisted as the necklace has been missing for too long a period. What shall we do now? Do you think the pawn broker, to whom you gave the necklace, will give us away?"

Her husband looked away worriedly. "Can't be sure of that. We must take back the jewellery from him and sell it off at an unknown place. But how do we get the money to buy it back from him? We'll need rupees ten thousand that we borrowed from him, plus the interest, to get the necklace released again."

"We know the necklace is worth almost a lakh of rupees. What if we take a loan of ten thousand from a moneylender, retrieve the necklace, and sell it at whatever price we get, which should be at least fifty thousand? And then repay the moneylender too. But we must have a ready buyer. No use holding on the necklace indefinitely, as the moneylender's interest will be very high."

Maya's husband removed the slip of paper the boy had given him in the street. What luck! He got down to planning the entire deal. He knew a person who would give him the loan at an exorbitant interest rate. But the loan would be for just a day. No harm done.

It was 3.30 PM and Karishma had taken up position next to a tea stall in front of the police station. The address Krishna had handed over to Maya's husband was just two houses away. It was a small house, old and unimpressive. A tailor's shop took up half of the ground floor, and an old man stood on the balcony on the only floor above. From her vantage point Karishma could keep an eye on both, the house as well as the police station. Through a window she could see her uncle, the police inspector, at his table, just as she had calculated.

Now it would be clear if the culprit was really Little Pinku as everyone thought, or Maya as she suspected.

4 o'clock it already was, and no sign of Maya or her husband. But she had given the time as between 4 and 5 pm. The wait had just begun.

4.15 pm and she started pacing up and down, between the two buildings. Mustn't get impatient, she admonished herself. Lots of time left yet.

4.30 pm and still no sign of either Maya or her husband. Was she wrong after all? Maybe they already have buyer, or maybe they have decided to come some other day? The possibility of 'another day', she struck out. She had taken care of that.

Suddenly, she saw her uncle come out of the police station and get into a waiting jeep. *Omigosh!!* If he goes away, the whole plan will go for a six. She ran forward and called out loudly to him.

"Karishma? What in the world are you doing here?" he was not in uniform she noted thankfully.

"Just visiting a friend when I thought I'd have a cup of tea with you."

"That's nice, but not today dear. I've just been called for a..."

"*Please!* It will take just a few minutes and they are supposed to make the best tea in town." She said pointing to a ramshackle stall.

"Really? Here I work right in front of the stall and I've never heard of its popularity. Okay, let's give it a try."

Five minutes later, the inspector put down his empty plastic cup and prepared to pay for the tea. Karishma frantically looked around for any sign of her prey, but there was none.

"I'd like one more cup, uncle. Please."

The inspector looked irritated. "Well okay, but frankly I wouldn't give this stall the reputation of serving the best tea in town. And why do you keep looking all round us? You have not paid attention to a word I've been saying."

It was 4.45 pm already, and Karishma was sipping her tea as though each drop had to be sipped separately. *No sign of her suspects yet.*

"Will you please finish that last sip so that I can be on my way?" cried her uncle, impatiently looking at his watch.

Then she saw him! Moving suspiciously, Maya's husband hovered around the entrance of the address she had given.

"There he is!"

"What...who?"

"Please trust me, uncle. I've laid a trap for this man. If my suspicions are correct this man will have a stolen necklace on him." Karishma pulled the inspector's arm urgently.

The totally bewildered inspector looked dumbly at her. "You laid a trap for...him, or me? You..."

"Please let's not waste time. He might run away when he realises he has been fooled." Karishma could be persuasive when she wanted to be, but today she was downright pushy.

They briskly walked up to Maya's husband as he stood talking to the tailor on the ground floor.

"Kalu?" the tailor was asking. "No one by that name in this house. In fact no one by that name in this locality."

"But...I am sure this was the address..."

"Why don't you ask the Inspector Sahib, behind you? He knows everyone here."

The man almost jumped out of his skin on hearing this. He whirled round, ready to run, but Karishma and her uncle had him cornered.

"Hand it over!" Karishma snapped, reassured by the presence of her uncle close by. "The game is up. We all know about the necklace."

Later, at the Chopra's residence, the two families had gathered for dinner. Mrs Chopra was clutching on to her necklace as though it was about to leap out of her hands.

"And to think I considered Maya to be totally trustworthy. And I kept blaming poor Little Pinku," she said, eyes lowered in shame. "But how did she do it, I am still not clear. Remember, she came only after the robbery was discovered."

"Earlier she had made a duplicate set of your house keys," explained Karishma, thoroughly enjoying the attention she was getting. "She also knew where you keep your jewellery, till it is returned to the bank locker. That night her husband, a petty thief, had sneaked into your house, taken the necklace from your drawer and made off without touching anything else, knowing next day with a little help from Maya, Little Pinku will be blamed."

"Why didn't they sell it immediately?" intervened Mr Chopra who had little idea of what had happened till date.

"That may have been dangerous," replied the inspector, also a guest at the dinner. "So they pawned it first, got whatever money they needed for the time being, and later when things had cooled down, they planned to retrieve it from the pawn broker and sell it. This process would have taken a long time. So instead of waiting for things to happen, Karishma forced the issue on them."

"I know," said Mrs Chopra shyly. "But when she asked me to tell Maya that we will be contacting the police soon, I had no idea what she had planned."

"Yes," the inspector confirmed. "They confessed that they first took a loan for a day, and retrieved the necklace from the pawn broker. They then tried to sell it to a known dealer but he didn't offer a good price, so Maya's husband brought it to the address given by Krishna. Teaches you, greed gets you nowhere."

Krishna, who was sitting next to Karishma leaned over and whispered to her, "But where is Mr Yash Chopra?"

"Later." Karishma turned to the others, "and we must not forget to thank Krishna without whose help this just wouldn't have been possible."

As everyone applauded, Krishna just sat there looking around him with a surprised and embarrassed look. He later leaned over again and softly asked his sister, "My help? What did I do?'

Before Karishma could reply, Mrs Chopra cut in, "I suppose it all ended well except that, I am now without a maid."

Mr Chopra suddenly announced, "Yes, it all ended well thanks to Karishma…er…and Krishna. If there is anything we can do for you in return, you have only to ask."

"As a matter of fact there is." Everyone looked towards Karishma in surprise. "As you all know Little Pinku's last rites were never performed in this house. I wish you would summon a priest and conduct the *antim kriya* prayer for the little boy's soul to rest in eternal peace."

The strange suggestion was met with silence as forks and spoons were put down. In all the excitement everyone had forgotten the little boy's innocent pranks, albeit after death, were taken advantage of.

"Chopra confirmed. "We shall feel honoured to have that privilege."

❑❑❑

by the same author

The Witches of Waitiki

68/-

pp: 176

These stories will grip the imagination of readers – young and old – right from page one. *The Witches of Waitiki* holds you spellbound till the end, wondering whether Rishi will be overcome by the witches' spell or not. Then comes The Third Connection, where over-inquisitive Karishma pursues the man who murdered three landlords. Will she end up as another victim of the killer? A Dog's Day Out tells the tale of how the kidnapped sister of a drug addict is rescued by, but naturally, their dog! The Cabin at Nizams is a sci-fi story that transports you into another dimension and the world of Tenkos and Domens. And Brahm's Symphony tells of a boy who never held a cricket bat but went on to coach and win for his team.

The Woman in White

80/-

pp: 144

After *The Witches of Waitiki*, here's another book to fire the imagination of all readers.

The first story, ***Much Ado About Nothing*** recounts how young Karishma unmasks criminals who have stolen the famous Kohinoor diamond.

The Woman in White is the adventure of four young boys who investigate a 'haunted' house and almost come to grief.

The Wonder Boy is the story of the dog Cocky and a gifted boy tackling a gang of poachers who are killing zoo animals in the jungle.

Two Buttons and a Pin narrates how teenager Rishi helps a poor boy Dhanu, who is being framed for attempted murder.

Two Hours of Doom is a sci-fi adventure where 10-year-old Shiv is teleported into 35th century India and a brush with death.

Tales, Folk Tales & Legends
GOOD BOOKS
SATISFACTION GUARANTEED
Affordable Prices
Tales of Gopal the jester
Full of Wit, Wisdom & Humour
गोपाल भांड के किस्से
60/- each
गोपाल भांड के अन्य किस्से
60/- each
भारतीय लोक कथाएं
Fascinating Folk Tales of India
50/- each
मनोरंजक परी कथाएं
Enchanting Fairy Tales
50/- each
Tenali Rama
60/- each
Tales of Tenali Rama
तेनालीराम के किस्से
60/- each
71 Golden Tales of Panchatantra
60/- each
Lav Kush
लव कुश
36/- each
PANDA
An imprint of Unicorn Books, Delhi
Quality reading for children...
Indian Tales & Global Tales, New Tales & Folk Tales, Fables, Legends & Mythology and books on growing up well, first told or retold by children's authors.
All Books in Full Colour
5 Volumes + Combined Edition Also available in Hindi
71 Golden Tales of Panchatantra
350/- H.B.
Animal Folk Tales from Around the World
36/- each
3 Volumes. Also available in Hindi
Other Story Books
Interesting Stories of Proverbs
72/-
In Colour
कहावतों की कहानियां
80/-
50 Moral Tales ...from The Gurukul
68/-
In Colour
कहावतें
In Colour
68/-
Ancient Tales of Wit, Wisdom & Humour
48/-
मुल्ला नसरुद्दीन
The Funniest Tales of Mullah Nasruddin
48/- each
50 Wittiest Tales of Birbal
48/-
Jataka Tales
48/-
अकबर बीरबल के किस्से
30/-
लघु अपराध कथाएं
30/-